You Are My Everything
Paperback Copyright © 2020 Lorhainne Ekelund
Editor: Talia Leduc

ISBN-13: 978-1989698143

Give feedback on the book at:
lorhainneeckhart@hotmail.com

Twitter: @LEckhart
Facebook: AuthorLorhainneEckhart

Printed in the U.S.A

YOU ARE MY EVERYTHING

The Friessens

LORHAINNE ECKHART

You Are My Everything

What happens when you get black-out drunk and wake up married to a woman you never met before?

Up and coming hockey rookie Michael Friessen has everything going for him: a future few could hope for, parents who are his everything… He doesn't want anything more until one weekend before he secures a spot with the Canucks, when he wakes up with a ring on his finger and the hottest, sexiest blonde sound asleep beside him.

He tries to tell himself it was a mistake, that he isn't looking for a relationship, and despite everything about her, including the night he's still trying to remember, he's determined not to fall for her. But the closer they get, the deeper he falls—until he learns that the night they met may not have been accidental.

"An unusual romance, with characterizations that are top notch."

Susan1

The Friessen Legacy Series Reading order:

The Outsider Series

The Forgotten Child (Brad and Emily)
A Baby And A Wedding
Fallen Hero (Andy, Jed, and Diana)
The Search
The Awakening (Andy and Laura)
Secrets (Jed and Diana)

Runaway (Andy and Laura)
Overdue
The Unexpected Storm (Neil and Candy)
The Wedding (Neil and Candy)

The Friessens: A New Beginning

The Deadline (Andy and Laura)
The Price to Love (Neil and Candy)
A Different Kind of Love (Brad and Emily)
A Vow of Love, A Friessen Family Christmas

The Friessens

The Reunion
The Bloodline (Andy & Laura)
The Promise (Diana & Jed)
The Business Plan (Neil & Candy)
The Decision (Brad & Emily)
First Love (Katy)
Family First
Leave the Light On
In the Moment
In the Family: A Friessen Family Christmas
In the Silence
In the Stars
In the Charm
Unexpected Consequences
It Was Always You
The First Time I Saw You
Welcome to My Arms
Welcome to Boston (A Paige & Morgan Short Story)
I'll Always Love You
Ground Rules

A Reason to Breathe
You Are My Everything
Anything For You
The Homecoming
When They Were Young (Link included FREE with The
Homecoming)
Stay Away From My Daughter
The Bad Boy
A Place of Our Own
The Visitor
All About Devon
Long Past Dawn
How to Heal a Heart

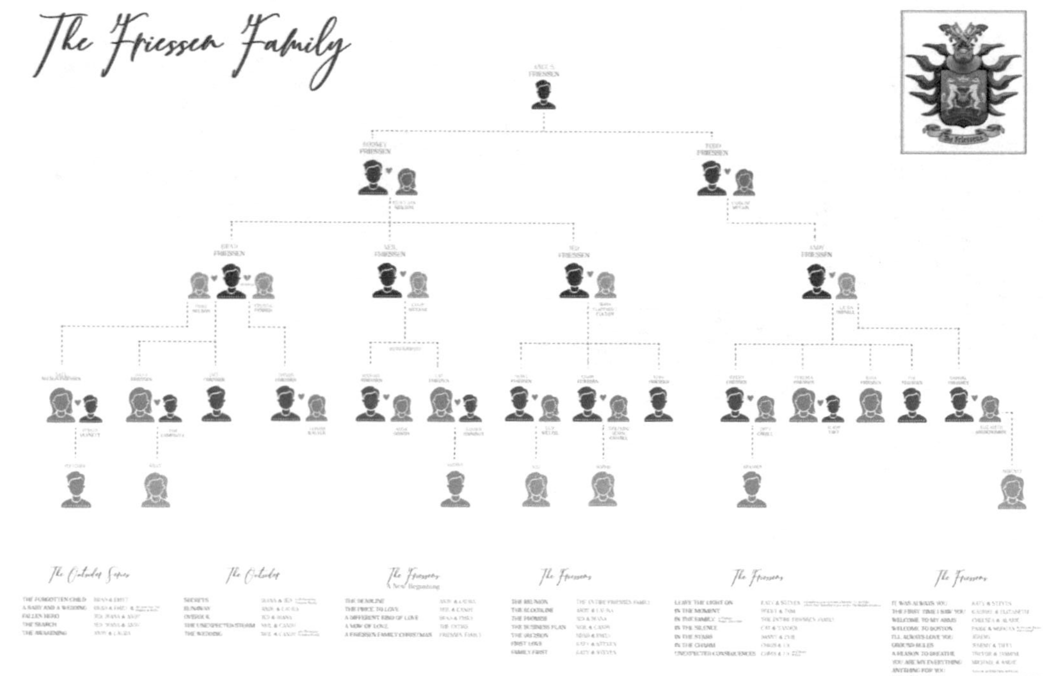

The Friessen Family

The Outsider Series
THE FORGOTTEN CHILD
A BABY AND A WEDDING
FALLEN HERO
THE SEARCH
THE AWAKENING

The Outsider
SECRETS
RUNAWAY
OVERDUE
THE UNEXPECTED STORM
THE WEDDING

The Friessens
A New Beginning
THE DEADLINE
THE PRICE TO LOVE
A DIFFERENT KIND OF LOVE
A VOW OF LOVE
A FRIESSEN FAMILY CHRISTMAS

The Friessens
THE REUNION
THE BLOODLINE
THE PROMISE
THE BUSINESS PLAN
THE DECISION
FIRST LOVE
FAMILY FIRST

The Friessens
LEAVE THE LIGHT ON
IN THE MOMENT
IN THE FAMILY
IN THE SILENCE
IN THE STARS
IN THE CHARM
UNEXPECTED CONSEQUENCES

The Friessens
IT WAS ALWAYS YOU
THE FIRST TIME I SAW YOU
WELCOME TO MY ARMS
WELCOME TO BOSTON
I'LL ALWAYS LOVE YOU
GROUND RULES
A REASON TO BREATHE
YOU ARE MY EVERYTHING
ANYTHING FOR YOU
THE HOMECOMING

Chapter One

How many times had he told himself it wasn't a good idea to close down the bar? It was even worse after a game, a win, a night out in a new town, when they just couldn't resist blowing off steam, or so their coach called it. Except tonight was different, considering it was his twenty-first birthday, and what had he done with his three besties from the team but driven across the border to Vegas?

Shit!

He'd have smiled and laughed if it didn't hurt so damn much.

Now here he was, unable to open his eyes past the thumping in his head—not the music from the club, no. Now as he lay there in his misery, it felt more like someone was ramming a hammer, or rather a sledgehammer, into his head. The pounding just wouldn't quit. He needed water and forced himself to lift a lid even though he felt as if ground-up glass had been scraped over his eyeballs as soon as he took in the bright sun streaming in through a window he didn't recognize. Right, a hotel room, of course.

White sheets were twisted around him, from what he could barely make out, and he didn't remember how he'd gotten there. He needed to move, but each muscle protested loudly, and his mouth tasted as if something had recently died in it.

Happy twenty-first birthday, Michael! He groaned and then immediately regretted it, as the pounding in his head was sickening.

Even thinking hurt as he tried to remember how many boilermakers he'd downed. Just thinking of the cheap whiskey with beer had him wanting to retch as he somehow managed to move his hand and then slide his naked ass to the edge of the bed. He shut his eyes and groaned again as he lowered his head to his hands, knowing that he was in deep shit. He still had practice and another game tomorrow, and right now he didn't know how he'd manage to walk, let alone pull on skates and race down the ice to play the game he loved. Calling in sick wasn't an option, not when he was on his way to the pros.

He forced himself to stand and squinted at the desert sun, feeling as though the sand was scraping his eyes all the way up where he was, at least twenty stories high. He looked down and took in the strip of Vegas, trying to remember where they had ended up and what hotel this was.

Nope, nothing. Just a haze of…well, what he was sure had been a great time.

"Water," he mumbled and staggered to the bathroom, where he turned on the tap and stuck his head under to drink what he could, then let the cold water run over his neck, his head, his face. *Ah, relief!*

He needed aspirin, a ton of it, then maybe coffee. He took in his bloodshot eyes and the five o'clock shadow he sported in the mirror as the water ran from his face. His short dark hair was sticking up, dripping beads of water, and he allowed the fact to sink in that he was now legal everywhere.

He'd have been excited if his head wasn't about to blow off—but he'd had fun, he thought, from what he could remember. He wiped his hand over his face, swiping away the beads of water, and caught a gleam of gold on his finger. He froze.

Like, what the fuck?

He just stared, and every muscle in his body tightened as he took in the ring. All manner of horror shot through him as he racked his brain, trying to remember what the hell he had done. A joke, a prank—had to be one of the guys, Stu, Kyle, or maybe Nathan. Yeah, Nathan was always pulling something. Geez, he hoped he hadn't dressed him up like a girl and taken photos while he was passed out, because that was exactly what one of them would do.

He stepped out of the bathroom and took in the bed, then froze again when he saw blond hair, the long blond hair of a woman who was naked and sound asleep on her stomach with the sheet covering her ass.

Like, double what the fuck?

She didn't move, and he took in the smallish room, for Vegas, seeing his clothes tossed everywhere: a shoe by the door, her bra hanging over a chair. He took a step and kicked a killer red heel, seeing a long slim leg sticking out from under the sheet. Where the hell were his friends? Another room, maybe. Like he could remember.

So he'd picked up a woman and had sex, and there was a ring on his finger. It hurt to think, because all he wanted to do was puke—whether from the fact that he could smell the booze oozing out of his pores or the fact that he couldn't remember what the hell he had done, he wasn't sure.

He reached for his pants and stumbled from the dizziness for a minute. After that nearly took him to his knees, he shoved his feet into his favorite blue jeans, which smelled ripe with stale beer, and turned around, feeling suddenly awkward, as if she were awake and sitting up, watching him as he zipped up his fly. This awkward, shy feeling was completely ludicrous, given the scenario.

He made his way over to the bed, taking in the silky black skirt and underwear on the floor, then the face of the blonde. Her mascara was smudged, her full red lips were parted slightly, and she was still sound asleep. So what were his options? Get dressed, slip out…and then what?

He pressed his hands to the mattress and shook, but nothing happened. He did it again, harder, and she stirred and pulled in a breath, then blinked and went to roll over before she spotted Michael staring down at her.

"What time is it?" Her voice was groggy, and she lifted her hand and brushed back her hair. She rolled over, pulling at the sheet and lifting it to cover herself, but not before he caught a glimpse of two perfectly round breasts. If he weren't so hungover, he might have appreciated the sight. Then he spotted a gold ring on her finger as she sat up and pulled her knees to her chest, maybe feeling some of the awkwardness he felt.

She reached for the clock by the bed. "Shit, it's after nine! You were supposed to set the alarm." Then she tossed back the covers, and her bare feet hit the beige carpet, her toenails painted a vibrant red. He stepped back, taking in her gorgeous naked body: fit, slim, and exactly the kind of woman he wanted in his bed. She stepped into her underwear and then her skirt and said something under her breath that he couldn't quite make out as she hurried across the room and reached for her bra. She pulled it on, and then she was on the floor, on her knees on the other side of the bed, looking for something.

"This may sound totally weird and all," Michael said, "but I must have drunk an awful lot last night, because I don't remember coming back here. As gorgeous as you are, we met where…?"

She was holding a deep auburn and black silky tank up over her bra as she sat back on her knees, her deep blue eyes staring at him with horror. Okay, maybe not too cool on his part, implying that he didn't remember her—but he didn't.

"I mean, if you could just fill me in, and then this here…" He lifted his hand, and the ring was the same plain gold as hers.

She was still looking at him, wide eyed, when she lifted the tank and pulled it on, then rose to her feet on the other side of the bed. Her long blond hair was a tangled mess as she took in her own hand, her own ring finger. "Well, that's kind of a problem, then, isn't it?" she said, and he sensed he'd hit a nerve.

"If I can't remember, then yeah, it is," he started, then stopped as she took a step around the bed and reached for a red heel by the door. "So…two rings, a bed, a hotel, and—"

She pulled in a breath and sighed. "I'm your wife."

Chapter Two

S he was walking out the door, her beautiful sexy ass swaying in that short silky skirt, and he was stuck on the horror of "wife"! At the same time, he could hear his phone buzzing from somewhere in the hotel room.

"Wait, what do you mean, we're married? This is impossible. There has to be some mistake, some sick joke. It was my birthday, and granted, I see that we slept together, and I'm sure it was fantastic…but married? No way. I…" He followed her out of the room, which was only two doors down from the elevator, where she was now standing. She had pressed the elevator button. He heard the door shut behind him and realized he didn't have a keycard.

A woman and some kids came out of another room across the hall, dressed for the pool, and there he stood, looking like shit. He spotted his image in the reflection of the elevator doors, and just one look told the story of too much booze, partying, and sex, all of which he also couldn't remember.

"Look, seriously, could you, like, wait? Give me a minute," he said.

The woman in the pastel floppy hat and her kids stared over to him and then over to his wife, whose name he didn't even know. This was insane.

He gestured, flexing his fingers before fisting them and pulling them back before he could touch her. Touching this stranger would be overstepping, even though he'd likely had his hands in all kinds of intimate places. Now, in the light of day, this sobering day, he was cursing every single idiotic, reckless thing he'd ever done.

"I don't even know your name, and we're, like, married?" he said. It sounded pathetic even to his own ears, and he didn't miss the way the mother at the elevator winced and shook her head.

"Only in Vegas," she muttered as the elevator door opened, and she and her kids stepped in. This time, he reached for the blonde's arm and touched it.

"Please, give me a minute."

She sighed and glanced over to his hand, which was still on her arm, holding her. He let go and lifted his hands to show her. He was feeling a hint of panic—to touch or not to touch her? He didn't have a clue. The elevator doors slid closed, and the blonde now faced him.

"I'm Michael..." he began.

"Yes, Friessen, Michael Friessen. I guess at least one of us knows the name of the person they married. You seriously don't remember?"

He still had enough sense to know when a woman was pissed. At least his brain could register that much, but then he had a moment where he wasn't sure if she was angry or sad or if it was just disbelief staring back at him from her blue eyes, which seemed far clearer than his. She drew her finger under her eye, wiping at the smudged mascara.

"Angie Debois, and now Friessen, I suppose, since, yes, we were married at the little white chapel on the strip. Impulsive, really. So yup, married, really, truly…" She unzipped her purse and pulled out a folded piece of paper, then proceeded to unfold it and hold it out to him. All he could do was stare at the official paper that said *Wedding Certificate* on top. "See? Here's my signature, your signature, and the officiator's signature at the bottom. You purchased the simple package, which included the gold bands, the music, and the hotel room."

She handed him the paper, and he stared at the signature, his signature, the illegible familiar scrawl, and for a second he wondered if this was where his friends were supposed to jump out and tell him it was all a big joke, and happy twenty-first. He'd kill them after he got over the relief.

She was still staring at him, and he couldn't get his tongue to move. He felt the icy chill of the air conditioning blasting on his bare chest as he lowered the paper and took in the face of the woman he'd married: hair a mess and mascara still flaking, with traces under her eyes.

"Okay, I can fix this," he said, "but first, I need a keycard for the door."

She just stared at him. Her expression, he thought, was one of distrust. He needed to call his friends, get some aspirin and coffee, and figure out why he couldn't remember what he'd done—though, obviously, he had picked up a woman and then married her! At the same time, he imagined the horror on the faces of his coach, his team members, and, worse, his mom and dad. There was no way he could explain any of this to himself, let alone anyone else.

"I have no room keycard. That was all you," she said

and turned away from him, then pressed the button for the elevator again.

"No, wait, seriously," he said. "Look, you can't run out after dropping a bomb on me like this. If we're married…"

The look she tossed him bordered on that of a woman who was quickly losing her patience, likely because he kept jamming both his feet into his mouth. He knew he was making a mess of this situation, as he couldn't seem to find the right words.

"Okay, we're married," he said. "I see that, so let's just go back in the room and talk. Seriously, just give me a minute. Let me get dressed, figure some shit out, make some calls…"

She was shaking her head as she strode to the mirror behind him and wiped at the mascara under her eyes. "No can do. I have a job, which I'm now late for, as you were supposed to set the alarm but didn't."

The elevator door opened, and this time he couldn't stop her from stepping in. He could feel himself going under again, drowning, unable to save himself. He pressed his hand to the door to hold it open. "Wait, a job?" he said. A dancer, a stripper, obviously, from one of the bars they'd stopped at the night before. "How am I going to reach you, get a hold of you?"

She jabbed the button in the elevator, but he was holding the door so it couldn't close, because he couldn't let her walk away. Being married to a woman he didn't know was his worst nightmare.

"Seriously, I'm late," she said. "I've got to go, Michael."

Why did he feel nothing for a woman he'd supposedly married and then had a lot of sex with? "Where do you work—which bar, hotel, club? Tell me, and I'll come by later. We'll talk, sort this out…" Then he needed to be back in Boise for practice.

She was shaking her head and made a rude sound. "I'm a kindergarten teacher, not a bar worker or whatever you're obviously thinking." She gestured, motioning for him to get out, and then she fished a pen out of her purse, pulled a card from her wallet, and scribbled a number on the back before she handed it to him. "Here is my number, but I have to go."

He took the card, a library card, and he stepped back out of the elevator, taking in her long slender legs, red shoes, and short skirt. The entire package screamed sex. He couldn't wrap his head around the fact that he had never met a kindergarten teacher who looked like a stripper.

The doors slid closed, and his image reflected back at him. It wasn't flattering: a half-dressed man locked out and stinking of booze and sex. He turned in the hall, seeing the closed door and knowing he'd have to go down to the front desk and somehow explain himself.

He jabbed the elevator button when he heard the rattle of the maid's cart at the end of the hall. He took in the dark-haired woman in a brown hotel staff uniform.

"Excuse me, miss," he said, and started moving, digging into each step, his bare feet on the remarkably clean patterned Berber carpet.

The maid stopped and turned to face him, holding towels and toilet paper. Her expression was blank. This was obviously a sight she'd seen before, as her gaze tracked him all the way from the elevators to where she stood.

"I locked myself out of my room, as you can see, half dressed," he said. "Could you…?" He gestured to his bare chest and down the hall. Her gaze slid down him and to his bare feet, then back up again.

She just shook her head. "Mm-hmm. Well, I guess. Which room are you in?" She pulled out her keycard, evidently a master key, and followed him back down the hall.

"Right here, 1702," he said.

She tapped the door, and the green light blinked before she pushed it open and stepped inside. "You need anything, towels, ice…?"

He walked back into the room, seeing his shirt on the floor and hearing the buzz of his phone, which he spotted in the corner against the wall. "No, thanks," he said and turned to see the door already swinging closed, the maid now gone. "Yeah, Vegas, evidently not one of your most brilliant ideas," he muttered to himself as he stumbled over a shoe and grabbed his phone, seeing Nathan's name. "Like, what the fuck?" he started, pressing the speaker button on his Android.

"Well, it's about fucking time," Nathan said. "Where the hell are you?"

He could hear the panic in his friend's voice. At the same time, he was taking in his image in the mirror. Shock reflected back at him. "So you don't know what happened?" he snapped. "I'm in a fucking hotel room. I don't know how the hell I got here and woke up with some chick in my bed, my head feels like it's about to blow off, and you're telling me you know nothing?"

He didn't even know what hotel he was at. He took in the desk and spotted the book of hotel services with the name MGM. He could hear laughing from the other end and could hear Kyle and Stu in the background.

"Seriously, dude, is that all?" Nathan said. "We've been shitting ourselves, trying to find you. You don't answer your phone, and you disappeared last night after I hit the craps table. Kyle was getting his own lap dance, and Stu said last he saw of you, you were going to take a piss." Then he was laughing again, and Michael squeezed the phone, wanting to pull each of them aside and grill them about what they had seen so they could help him fill in the blanks, but he said nothing. "So get your ass together," Nathan said. "We have to get back, or coach is going to have our ass. Get rid of the babe. Where are you?"

He shook his head, because Angie wasn't just a babe. "At the MGM, room 1702," he said before ending the call, knowing he'd left out the biggest and most important part of the scenario, which was something he was still trying to wrap his head around: the fact that he was married.

Chapter Three

"So tell me again what happened," Kyle said, driving his six-year-old red four-door Subaru as they raced for the border after picking up Michael. He'd had time to shower, raid the minibar stash of aspirin, and order coffee from room service, at least.

Stu was in the passenger side, holding the wedding certificate Michael had handed them as they left the hotel after giving him a lecture that boiled down to "What the fuck?" "Holy shit," and "Seriously, dude, you really screwed the pooch big time." Worse was the sobering thought that they really hadn't known about any of it, the woman, the marriage, and how stupidly drunk he'd managed to get.

"Are you sure this isn't fake?" Stu tilted the paper sideways as if trying to verify it from a different angle, and Nathan reached around and ripped it from his hand from where he sat in the back seat with Michael. At least he didn't want to puke anymore after downing the greasy burger they'd picked up at the drive-thru. At the same time, he was ready to make a pact that he'd never pick up a drink again.

"Told you already, I woke up with the ring on my finger and can't remember shit—not when we met, where, the bars we went to… It's a big ol' blank, and I certainly don't remember the chapel and getting hitched. Fuck!" he said again, losing track of the number of times he'd dropped the F bomb since waking up to this nightmare that morning.

"Yeah, I don't know. Looks legit to me," Nathan said. "Seriously, you don't know her? Please tell me she isn't a dog."

He wanted to smack Nathan, who was no longer laughing. Now that the shock had worn off after he told them of his predicament, they'd realized he was serious. "She's a kindergarten teacher," Michael said. "Have some respect, would you? And no, apparently even in my blackout drunk state, I still have some taste. She's attractive, pretty."

No—hot, sexy, and how many miles back now? He didn't have a clue what he was going to do.

"A kindergarten teacher!" they all said in unison, and he shut his eyes, because the pounding in his head, which had only just subsided from a sickening thud to a nagging burn, was crawling up the back of his neck again. He leaned his head back, thinking of Angie and her expression of disbelief, and he couldn't help feeling like a dog, running her out without a word. It was ludicrous, considering he didn't know her. A stranger. Angie Debois-Friessen!

"Oh, shit," he said under his breath.

A hand slapped his chest. "We're just razzing you," Nathan said. "Listen, when we get back, after the game, you get a hold of a lawyer and get them to take care of this, an annulment. Should be easy. I mean, how many idiots have done the same thing, a quick trip to the altar in Vegas and they wake up in the morning wondering, holy shit, what did I just do? You'll fix it, get rid of the babe, and chalk it up to a birthday memory you'll never forget."

Michael flicked open his eyes, taking in Nathan's arrogance. He'd made it all sound as if it were no big deal, as if he'd bought the wrong color shirt. It was crazy, and maybe if he could think that way, feel that way, the situation wouldn't be bothering him the way it was now.

"Wake me up when we get there," he said and closed his eyes, leaning his head back, because this back-and-forth talking about how stupid he'd been wasn't helping.

He didn't know how long he slept, but a hand nudged him awake.

"We're here," Nathan said. "Shake a leg. We've got enough time to grab gear and hit practice…"

He fumbled his seatbelt and stepped out of the car, which was parked outside the Franklin Inn, where the rest of the team was staying.

"Michael!"

He looked up to see his dad, Neil, with a big smile, walking his way. His dark hair was mixed with gray, and he wore dark pants and a leather jacket. His mom, Candy, was there too, with her long dark hair pinned back, dressed casually in blue jeans, also with a big smile.

"Hey, Mom, Dad. Seriously, I didn't know you were coming…" He jerked his head over his shoulder, seeing Nathan, Stu, and Kyle already through the hotel doors.

"Oh my God, you stink!" his mom said as she hugged him. She made a face as she pulled back. "You're wearing the bar."

"Sorry, it was kind of a crazy night." He winced and

groaned, because he didn't have time for this or the explanation he hoped he'd never have to give.

"Kind of thought you'd be out with the guys, celebrating your twenty-first," his dad said. "We showed up last night and were told the four of you were out on the town. I guess that answers my question. Twenty-one, and you drank your way through it. You look like shit, but I hope you had fun."

He wondered if his dad would still be wearing that smile when he found out what he'd really done. "Yeah, it, uh…was a night, one I won't forget," he added, then gestured with his thumb to the hotel. "Got practice, and coach is going to kick our ass 'cause we're late." He took a step back and took in the way his mom glanced over to his dad. They were so happy, and he loved them. He bumped the car and nearly stumbled.

"Hey, take it easy there," Neil said. "Listen, I wasn't supposed to tell you this, but because you're looking ridiculously rough… The scouts are here. Coach called me, because they're interested in you."

For a second, Michael just stared at his dad, wondering if he'd heard right. "The scouts? The NHL scouts are here? But it's not even the draft," he stated. This wasn't the right time for everything he had ever wanted to happen.

His dad gestured to the hotel. "You'd better get going, grab your gear—and water. Drink lots to flush that booze out of you. I can smell it from here. Now's not the time to get benched when you've worked this hard to shine. We'll see you at the arena."

Neil and Candy walked away, and Michael silently kicked his own ass for thinking that driving to Vegas to celebrate the big twenty-one would in any way be a good idea.

I t was the third time her phone had rung—the third time in the past hour, that was, as she tidied up the toys into their bins and put away the art supplies for her afternoon kindergarten class. The last of the parents had walked out the door with their kids, but there had been none of the usual drama, with a few tears, some squeals of delight, and the general energy of kids who had been contained too long in a room during story time.

She still couldn't believe what she'd done. After racing home and hopping into a quick shower, she had changed into capris and a sleeveless blouse, ultra conservative, then raced to work and apologized to the principal, who'd filled in for her while she ran an hour late. If they only knew what she had done and where she had been.

She stared at her bare hand, absent the gold band, but reached into her pocket and pulled it out when her cell phone rang again. This time she picked it up from her desk, taking in the name display: M. Friessen. Great, her husband was calling.

She pulled in a breath. "Hello?" She waited, hearing a lot of background noise.

"Hey, uh, it's Michael. Is this Angie…the kindergarten teacher?"

Boy, awkward.

"Hi, Michael. Yes, it's me," she added, squinting. Just hearing his deep voice again in the light of day gave a little tug at her heart. What was wrong with her? She barely knew him, even though she had let him see a side of her she showed no one. Not that he remembered. He sighed, and she wondered what noise she was hearing.

"Hey, listen," he said. "I'm feeling kind of bad about all this, and especially this morning. It was awkward, not to mention that I'm sorry about how I reacted, considering the circumstances and all…"

She smiled to herself, because the horror she'd seen reflected on his face, in his eyes, when he realized they were actually married was something she'd been trying to come to terms with all day. During a night at the bar with her alter ego, as she called it, she had become that person she was never allowed to be during the day. She breathed and settled her hand over her other arm just as her boss and the school principal, Erin Brown, poked her head in and gestured, tapping her watch.

"Well, I guess it was for me, too. Um, listen. I'm just finishing up at work, but I can meet you…" She tucked the gold ring back in her pocket and nodded to her boss, knowing the staff meeting was about to start shortly.

"Yeah, about that," he started, and she could hear something in his voice that had her shutting her eyes—that hesitation. "I'm not in Vegas anymore."

Her stomach pitched with an awful hollow feeling. Things were going from bad to worse, and nothing seemed to be working out. "I see. Well, at least you called to let me know."

"No, listen, it's not that or what you're thinking it is. Look, last night was a celebration of sorts, for me, and I guess I got wasted and then ended up picking you up and getting married. Still don't know how it happened. I know this isn't an excuse, and I don't mean for it to sound that way. Since I can't really remember, but it's done, and we're married, we need to talk. I had an…appointment." He had hesitated, and she wasn't sure why. "But I'll be free after tomorrow. I can drive back down and see you, and we can…talk."

She could hear a lot in the background and wasn't sure what it was, the sounds, the noise, the voices. "Okay, so we'll talk," she said. "Listen, I really do have to go. Why don't you call me when you're coming back, and we'll get together?" She cringed at the way it sounded and said a quick goodbye before disconnecting, then gave her head a shake before pulling the gold ring from her pocket again, seeing what she'd done.

This was the girl she didn't let out, the one she didn't let anyone see. She shoved the ring back in her pocket and took in the clock. Right now, she was Angie Debois, Miss Debois, respectable, reliable, and the kind of woman who was entrusted to teach young minds. If anyone knew the truth, she would no longer be a teacher.

Chapter Five

He needed a minute to pull his head together. Hearing her voice again had only added to how off he was. He'd been slow at practice, from the battle drills to the cross-ice games. On any other night, he'd have loved to work on those skills. One of his strengths was being able to read and react and make quick decisions when waiting a second too long could cost them the game—but not tonight.

Good thing it had been only a practice, a practice that he had totally fucked up, going from the star player to just one of the rookies. The scouts watching had to have wondered why they'd heard he was such a superstar, because what they had seen was exactly the opposite.

Even his coach had pulled him aside and dressed him down, and then there was his dad, whom he'd caught a glimpse of behind the safety glass. By the way Neil watched him while he worked a piece of gum, Michael knew all too well he had a few things to say. His dad had even made his way over to the scouts, likely to smooth everything over.

This hangover was about to bring him to his knees, even without having to wrap his head around the thought of Angie, his wife. He held his cell phone just outside the locker room, all sweaty and stinking because the booze was still oozing out of him. At least the pounding in his head had stopped. He tried to get her voice out of his head.

"So what's going on?" Neil said, though Michael hadn't even heard him come up behind him. "Can't say I've ever seen you so out of it, even with a hangover. You missed everything out there, every shot on goal. You missed the pass just like a rookie. Don't think those scouts out there didn't catch it."

He wiped his forehead, hearing the echo from the arena, where his team was still practicing—but not him. He'd needed to figure out how to pull it together, so he'd called Angie. He didn't miss the way his dad glanced to his phone and then to his stick and helmet against the wall. His gloves were tossed on the floor.

What was he supposed to say? "It's complicated…" he started, but he had to stop himself from saying more. His dad wouldn't buy a line like that, and he stared over at Michael with a hard gaze that said he wasn't going to give him a pass.

"Really? In what way is it complicated, and does it have anything to do with your night out last night?"

He wondered whether his dad could read his mind. For a second, he could feel the concrete he was standing on give a little, because the way his dad was staring at him, watching him, he was sure he knew or had some idea of the trouble he'd gotten himself into—or maybe he was just being paranoid.

"Not answering?" Neil said and glanced to the side, taking in the pipes and the door to the locker room. "The scouts are ready to pack it in and leave, but I talked to them, because there's an offer on the table from the Canucks, and right now you're blowing it. Let me tell you, it took some talking to get them to stay. At your game tomorrow, you will shine."

Neil was pissed, and Michael would've had to be a fool to miss the demand. At least it wasn't his coach talking, because he wouldn't have been talking but yelling.

The Canucks? Like, holy shit, he'd known it was coming, but right now he couldn't get his head into the excitement of something he'd worked for his entire life.

"Don't yell," Michael finally said, and Neil stiffened, giving him everything in a glance.

"Why would I yell?" he said, then gestured for Michael to keep talking. He seemed to really dig into his stance.

"Because I did something really stupid last night," he said. How would his dad react to something he still couldn't get his head around?

"And that is…? Come on, Michael. I can see that whatever this is, it's eating you up. I've never seen you blow anything the way you are tonight. Whatever it is, it can't be that bad—"

"I got married."

Neil merely blinked as if he hadn't heard him, or maybe he had, judging by the confusion and the moment of silence. This never happened to his dad, ever!

"I drank too much, and I woke up this morning in a hotel on the strip in Vegas with a woman and a ring on my finger. I don't remember any of it," he said, then fisted his hand and rapped the concrete wall, and his dad stared at him with an expression he'd never seen before. Michael lifted his phone. "I'm just trying to figure out what the hell to do."

He could hear what sounded like the entire team coming down the hall to the locker room. As each one passed, they slapped him on the back or the shoulder, tossing out "Happy birthday!" along with all kinds of rude comments.

When they were gone and the locker room door closed, his dad rested his hand on his shoulder, twisted his mouth in a way he did when he was contemplating something, and said, "Get cleaned up and changed. I'll be out front."

Then he left, and Michael didn't know what to make of it other than to know his dad would be sticking his nose into every part of this major fuckup. He should've been happy at the thought of his dad fixing everything—but this was Neil Friessen, whose way of fixing things was often wildly different than what Michael wanted.

Chapter Six

"Look, this is the third time you've done this to me," Angie said. "I'm pretty sure you can't get away with this."

The landlords who owned the condo where she lived, Lou and Breanna Redmond, stood in her doorway. They had jacked up the rent every forty-five days since they'd purchased the condo earlier that year.

"This is market rent," Lou said, "and because we live in a capitalist country, we have every right to charge what we want. You either have the money to pay, or you need to pack up and leave, because there's a line of people around the block waiting to rent a place like this and pay the price I've set."

The Redmonds had taken the approach of getting their tenants to pay the mortgage for them by charging outrageous rents so they could, as they'd put it, come out way ahead. It was a win-win for them and a lose-lose for her. Since they'd purchased the condo she was renting, they had nearly tripled her original rent. Worse, she hadn't been able to find anything else that was even remotely affordable on a teacher's salary from the slim stock available in Las Vegas.

"This is highway robbery," Angie said. "You want another four hundred and fifty dollars, why?" She stared at the five-day notice, which stated she could either pay the rent or leave her two-bed, two-bath condo. The Redmonds looked like the kind of people everyone would invite to their backyard barbecue, but all she saw were a couple of extortionists in disguise. They'd been prepared to serve her notice when they came calling to collect the rent.

"Taxes have gone up, water bills, interest rates—you name it," Breanna said. "Unfortunately for you, when our costs go up, we have no choice but to pass it on to you. It's just the way it works when you rent a place. You can either find a way to reach out to the powers that be to see that our tax bill is lowered, or you can pay the rent with the skyrocketing costs the fleecing bureaucrats keep tacking on to us."

Were they serious? How was any of that on her? "Kind of the pot calling the kettle black, isn't it?" Angie said. "I can't afford this. I'm just a teacher with a teacher's salary…" She tapped the notice, feeling drained. Drinking a little too much the night before had sapped away her energy, but the living nightmare she was holding in her hands had brought on a lot of sleepless nights. The rental market in Vegas had all but dried up.

In a last Hail Mary, she held out a check in her sweaty palms for the old rent, but what did they do but just shake their heads, the smug bastards? She silently wished every manner of horrible thing to befall them.

"This is all I have," she said. "I sold my car last month. Any more and I won't be eating, and I still need to pay for power. As it is, I'm frequenting the hotels on the strip for their free appies and shrimp cocktails…" And their drinks, but she wasn't about to add that part. "Look, I'm just a teacher, and this isn't fair. At least give me some time to find another place."

They were still shaking their heads. "The full amount now, or we'll be changing the locks and putting your things out on the curb in five days," Lou said, shoving his hands in his pockets. "As we're the property owners, the law is on our side, so what will it be? Last chance."

She wondered if there was even a tiny bit of compassion in them. She stared from one to the other, but all she saw was hard and unforgiving. *Bastards!* She just shook her head, feeling the quiet desperation that had been clawing at her moments earlier become the realization that she couldn't keep fighting off the inevitable. She allowed her hands to fall to her sides.

"Well, then I guess we've said all we need to say," Lou said. "Please see to it that you vacate promptly, and be sure to clean the unit as well. Consider your deposit gone, because it will be needed to cover the days you owe, for our time to rent the place again, and for any damages there may be."

There wasn't even a shred of decency as they took Angie in one more time before they walked down the four concrete steps to the street. The neighborhood was two blocks from the strip and three from the school where she worked, and she didn't have a clue what she was going to do.

As she closed the door, she had to settle her hand over her stomach, as she felt a trembling that seemed to start right in her center and shoot outwards. Shock, stress, more sleepless nights…

She squeezed the door handle, taking in the condo where she'd lived for nearly two years: the small kitchen, the open living room, and the stairs that went up to the second floor master. She'd even amassed some furniture. How would she do this? Where could she move? What would she do with everything she owned?

Then there was Michael, another mess, another situation she hadn't allowed herself a moment to consider. She shoved her hand in her pocket and pulled out the simple gold band, remembering all too well the night before at the hotel and the freebie casino vodka soda she'd been drinking when he slipped onto the stool beside her—drunk, gorgeous. A bar and a club later, when her guard was down, Angie, the fun girl, had been hanging all over him, drenched in a copious amount of booze, and he'd been slipping a ring on her finger.

She strode into the kitchen and rested the ring on the island beside her cell phone, considering her situation. She was married to a man she didn't know. In an ideal situation, her husband would be the first one she called in her predicament, but he was a stranger, and she wasn't sure where he even was or if she'd hear from him again.

Her options were bleak. Unless she found a place in five days, she would join the ranks of the homeless who were growing in vast numbers in the city. As she leaned on the counter, considering her options, she realized that being married to Michael Friessen, the hockey star, could be her only salvation.

Chapter Seven

H e reminded his parents he wasn't two years old as he
found himself sitting on the sofa in the living room
of the hotel suite his parents had booked. Add in the fact
that Stu, Nathan, and Kyle were also there, and the
spacious suite was now bordering on overcrowded.

Kyle was leaning against the mantle of the fireplace,
and Stu and Nathan were sitting in the two easy chairs, all
showered and freshly changed into blue jeans and faded T-
shirts. After the shower, Michael could feel that the booze
that had been seeping from his pores was on its way out.

His mom was sitting beside him, holding a glass of red
wine that his dad had poured her, wearing knee-high boots
over jeans and a flowing white and blue gypsy blouse. He
couldn't get over the fact that she seemed unusually calm,
considering his dad was on the phone, pacing back and
forth in the bedroom, speaking with his lawyer.

Michael lifted the bottle of water to his lips and took a
swallow, aware that his dad hadn't offered any of them a
beer—not that he'd have taken one. The way he was still

feeling, booze would certainly stay off his list of things to drink for now.

"What's her name?" Candy said. She took in each of them before letting her gaze land on him. Between his parents, his mom hadn't said much, and he wasn't sure what to make of it, this quiet calm.

"Uh…Angie."

Kyle was shaking his head and now thumbing through his cell phone. He was clearly listening but didn't look Michael's way.

"And you didn't know her," Candy said. It wasn't a question, and the way his mom locked her deep brown eyes on him, he wondered whether a lecture was coming.

"No, and I'm kicking myself already over what happened—but seriously, I mean, I can't remember even meeting her. I've never blacked out before…" He stopped talking, as his mom raised a brow and glanced over to his dad, who was standing in the doorway, watching them. It was unnerving, as if she had a sixth sense that he was there.

She lifted her chin, and he noted the way his dad glanced from him to his mom. "Good news, bad news, or…" Candy started and then glanced his way again.

"Apparently, 'got drunk and made a mistake by getting married in Vegas' is not solid legal grounds for an annulment," Neil said, "likely because of the carefree attitude that comes over people when they hit Vegas and the sheer number of wedding chapels where drunk idiots do the same dumbass thing."

Michael squeezed the plastic of his water bottle and heard the crack, and everyone decided then to stare at him as if all agreeing to his dad's point. Fine, he was an idiot. He'd be the first to admit that, and he'd kick his own ass as soon as he could remember at which point he'd lost the ability to see reason and thought it was in any way a good idea to get married to some broad he'd picked up. Where exactly he'd met her was a question he still needed an answer to.

"So he's stuck with the chick, then. Is that what you're saying?" Kyle tossed out over his shoulder, all the while acting as if he and his dad were the ones trying to save his ass.

"No, didn't say that, but it was enlightening, to say the least, to hear that even impulsive Vegas weddings aren't easy to make go away. In fact, to get a Vegas marriage annulled, you have to prove at least one of the following: that there was fraud or that you married someone underage."

Michael had to pause at the thought of Angie being underage. "Uh, she said she's a kindergarten teacher, so I can't see that one applying. She didn't look underage."

His dad just shook his head. "Well, you can be grateful for that much, because that would've created a much larger problem for you. The only other possibility is if she's married to someone else already, which, considering how this is going, may be a reach, or if you were mentally incompetent or unable to understand what you were consenting to. If you were so drunk you can't even remember marrying her, that's likely the best route to plan for an annulment." Neil glanced over to Stu and Nathan and then to Kyle. "Which one of you was supposed to be keeping an eye on him?"

Even he could feel the way the tension ratcheted up.

Nathan lifted his hands. "I told you both I was going to the craps table and to keep an eye on him, so that wasn't on me. He was already shitfaced, and I was done with that strip club and headed over to the Flamingo."

"Hey, it's not as if he's a kid," Kyle said. "We were

having a great time at a gentlemen's club, drinking, celebrating. He was at the table with you, Stu—since I was kind of preoccupied," he added, then cleared his throat, taking in Candy.

Yeah, this was something he didn't want to talk about in front of either of his parents: the women, the strippers, the fun.

"Preoccupied with what?" Neil said, sounding pissed as he stared over at Kyle. Michael could see this could become damn embarrassing.

"We should probably not disclose everything, considering where we were," Kyle said. "I mean, no offense, Mrs. Friessen, but it was a strip club, and I'm a guy, and…"

"Stop talking. This is my mom," Michael snapped. Neil just lifted his gaze to the ceiling, evidently understanding.

"You think I don't have a pretty clear idea of what you all were doing?" Candy finally said and let her gaze land on him.

"Okay, so booze, women, and trouble," Neil said, taking them all in. "Add in some gambling, and how about this woman my son married? Where did you meet her?"

All they did was look at each other.

"Well, that's the thing," Stu said. "The last time I saw Michael was at the strip club. He said he was going to take a piss—uh, sorry…go to the bathroom."

Candy looked as though she was doing her best to hide her amusement.

"So you're saying you never saw this woman?" Neil asked, and Michael was still trying to remember the club, the bathroom, but there was nothing. "What I can't understand is if he was so stinking drunk and wandered off to the bathroom, why didn't one of you go with him?"

That was the first time he'd seen his friends speechless.

"Because, Dad," Michael said, "it wasn't the first time

we hit the town and drank ourselves under the table. I didn't need a sitter to take a leak. Sorry, Mom," he added. She reached over and patted his leg but said nothing. "The real issue is how to fix this, not getting me to rehash a night I can't remember." He leaned forward, resting his forearms on his knees, picturing the gold band he'd woken up wearing just that morning tossed in his bag along with his dirty clothes.

"You want it straight?" Neil said, which was odd, considering he didn't give it any other way. Michael just stared at him, but he didn't answer, so his dad leaned his shoulder against the bedroom door frame. "If you and this woman you married want an annulment and you get her to agree to sign all the paperwork with no fuss, then it'll take as little as a few days, and it'll be done, over, and you can then both walk away. It's straightforward and easy—but, and this is a big 'but' that could throw a wrench into everything and cause a huge pain in your ass, if she decides she doesn't want the marriage annulled and you can't prove your inability to remember, then the process becomes something more drawn out, more expensive. If it drags out, it'll come down to you trying to get a divorce."

He took in his dad and everything he had just laid out to him, and he didn't know what to say, because he didn't know Angie, nothing about her—how old she was, where she lived, what she liked and didn't like…everything a man should know about the woman he married.

"So I'll talk to her, get her to agree to sign the papers," Michael said, and he wasn't sure why his dad was staring at him as if he'd said the stupidest thing ever.

"You think it will be that easy?" Neil said, not pulling his gaze from his son. It was so intense that it had Michael wanting to slip out of the room. He knew there was more to come and he likely wasn't going to want to hear it.

"Never said it would be easy, but I'll deal with it."

Yeah, from the expression on his dad's face, that definitely wasn't something he wanted to hear. "You mean like how you dealt with getting yourself into this? No, I think maybe I'll have a word with her, because in case you didn't realize it, Michael, you're now one of the hottest catches around, on your way to the pros." His dad scanned them all as if letting his point sink in. "Did any of you even consider the fact that this woman might've already known who you were and set her sights on you? The wife of an NHL player… I'm betting there may be more to this than you realize."

Michael just stared at his dad and then at his friends with a sinking feeling, hoping his dad was just trying to scare the shit out of him—because if that was the case, it was working.

Chapter Eight

Her prospects were slim, considering she was still paying off a mountain of student loan debt from her teaching degree, and her job provided only a passable income and wasn't getting her any closer to her dream of owning her own home. Worse, renting was now also reaching a point of unaffordability, since there was nothing even remotely in her price range. She wouldn't be able to afford the first and last month or the damage deposit, since she wasn't about to see a cent of what she'd already paid back.

How was this even possible? She was going to have to pick up a second job or maybe consider leaving the state and finding a new job at a new school in a place she could afford. But none of that would help her in her current situation, considering the clock was ticking and she had basically two days to come up with the deposit for a new place.

Option two, which was becoming a reality, would be to sell off some of her furniture, rent a storage locker for everything she couldn't sell…and then what, sleep in the car she no longer had? She couldn't rely on her family. Her sister was going through her second divorce in Des Moines, her father lived outside Mobile in a trailer park, and she didn't have a clue where her brother was now. On a rig someplace, she thought, in the middle of the Atlantic or the Pacific. One of the oceans, anyway.

Nope, she was basically on her own.

Then there was Michael.

"Right," she said as she looked in the bathroom mirror at the plunging neckline of her sleeveless auburn blouse. It showed an indecent amount of cleavage, and add in the short black skirt, knee-high boots, and extra coating of mascara on her smoky shadowed eyes, and she was no longer Miss Debois but Angie Debois, who turned heads the minute she walked into the hotel casinos.

She looked especially hot tonight and planned to hit Caesars or the Luxor, get a few drinks, some free appetizers to feed her, and… Her cell phone buzzed, and she took in the screen, seeing the name M. Friessen. Just seeing his name had her palms sweating and her stomach doing a flip.

"Hello?" she answered, staring at herself in the mirror, seeing a kindergarten teacher who couldn't be spotted like this.

"Angie, it's Michael. Sorry it took me so long to get back to you, but I plan on coming back to Vegas so we can meet. The plan was tomorrow, but something's kind of come up, so I'm coming back tonight instead. Actually, I'm already on my way."

She just stared in the mirror, hearing her heart hammering in her ears. Even the pull of her breath seemed to echo. "So you'll be here when?" She let her hand settle over her stomach, which rumbled, knowing there was nothing in the fridge to eat.

· "Less than an hour, give or take. I'm flying in this time, as I have to be back fast. How about meeting at the airport, and we'll sit and have a talk?"

Sure, if only she had a car. "Well, that's kind of a problem, since I don't have a car." She winced, wondering what he'd say.

"Okay, no problem. I'll rent a car or take a cab from the airport. Give me your address."

She stepped out of the bathroom, taking in her unmade bed and the boxes she'd tossed in the corner to start packing. She rattled off her address, picking up the clothes she'd stepped out of and left in a pile all over her bedroom floor.

"So you'll be here in about an hour?" she said, and she could hear an announcement in the background. He was already at the airport.

"Give or take," he said. "Listen, I've got to go. We're just boarding. Talk to you soon."

Then he hung up, and she was stuck on the fact that he'd said "we." Who was coming with him?

She didn't like mysteries, yet here she was, living in one of her own creation. Angie quickly tucked the boxes into the spare room and closed the door, then cleaned up her bedroom, deciding to change the sheets for a fresh pair. She cleaned the bathroom, the living room, and the unused kitchen, then ran the vacuum and was just putting it away in the closet when she heard a knock at the door, which instantly had her heart hammering. She made herself take a last look at her now neat and tidy place, which she would have to leave in two days, and walked to the door, silently berating herself for feeling so nervous.

She pulled in a breath and let it out before opening the door and seeing Michael—tall, ripped, dark haired, and more handsome than she remembered. And he was sober.

Beside him was an older man who resembled Michael

and wore a look that said he wasn't about to be messed with.

Yeah, okay, so this was the "we."

HOLY GOOD GOD, she was smoking hot. That silky number that was supposed to be a shirt left little to the imagination as to what a killer body she had, and her mile-long legs were bare under a very short black skirt. It took him a second to find his tongue and put a reasonable thought together, as the only one that stuck in his head was *This is my wife.*

"You must be Angie Debois," Neil said, holding out his hand the way he did, taking control right from the get-go.

Michael took in the startled edge Angie did her best to hide. It was just something that was there for a second in her eyes as she looked from him to his dad and slowly held out her hand.

"Sorry, this is my dad," Michael said, "Neil Friessen."

"Um, nice to meet you. Come in." She sounded frazzled, and he didn't miss the way his dad tossed him a look over his shoulder as he stepped inside—both a warning and a hint that he was likely to hear about this for a good many years to come. Michael was sure the lecture would have included words like "sexy" and "trouble."

Angie now had a smile pasted to her lips, but her eyes gave away how nervous or maybe tense she was. He stepped inside and rested his hand on her bare arm.

"Hey, um, even considering all this…you look nice," he said, which was not what he'd meant to say. He had to wonder if this was how she dressed or if it was just for him.

Blue eyes flicked up to him, and he took in her long blond hair, which hung in soft waves and added to the package. He was still having trouble seeing a kindergarten teacher in all this.

"Thank you," she said. "I guess I didn't realize you were bringing your father, although when you said 'we' on the phone, I wondered. I'm assuming this isn't an intimate talk for two?"

He picked up her sarcasm as he glanced over his shoulder to see his dad in the living room, looking around. Neil wasn't shy and was all about solving problems himself even when they weren't his to solve.

"Sorry, he insisted on coming," Michael said. "I humored him."

He allowed his gaze to linger and then let it run down her body, taking in all of her. It was bold and could get him slapped, but he wasn't sure what the protocol was for a woman who was his wife but a stranger. He caught the gold band on her finger as she closed the door, and for a second he couldn't shake the feeling her expectations might be different than his. Seeing that ring on her finger had him wondering if she saw the marriage not as a drunken mistake but as something she was going to stick with.

He could feel his hands sweat, so he stepped into the living room, taking in the cute light sofa and easy chair, the browns and creams, the simple touches, tasteful and far from flashy. It was neat and tidy and led to an open kitchen with two bar stools and dark cabinets.

His wife was looking from him to his dad, an open question on her face.

"We may as well get right to it," Neil stated, and Michael immediately wanted to stop him from cutting right through the bullshit.

"Let's sit down," he said and gestured to Angie. He couldn't look his dad's way because he knew he was glaring daggers at him.

Angie strode over to the sofa and took a seat at the end. Her short black skirt rode up, and it wasn't lost on him that her thighs were a work of art.

"So how was work? You teach kindergarten, right?" Michael said, joining Angie on the sofa, a cushion between them. He tried to ease the tension that had ratcheted up in the room by flashing one of his killer smiles, but he heard his dad clear his throat and didn't miss the way Angie glanced over to him. Neil was now sitting in the chair opposite them, a glass-topped sofa table between them.

Angie pulled in a breath and crossed her legs, resting her hands over her knee. "Yes, I am a kindergarten teacher, but I'm guessing you're not here to talk about my job."

"You're right about that," Neil said. "We're here to talk about how to fix this mess my son has found himself in, so we should get right to it. The best way to fix this is an annulment. Since Michael can't remember even marrying you, there's the matter that he wasn't of sound mind to consent, with all the drinking that was going on. Drunken beyond reason is an understatement. Let's make this quick and easy. You agree to sign the papers and make this go away, this mistake of a marriage, which I'm sure you'll agree—"

"Dad," Michael interrupted, as he hadn't missed the way Angie stiffened. His dad was trying to make it out as if this were all on her, even though he still couldn't figure out how and where he'd met her and how he'd ended up married to her.

"Angie, look…" He leaned forward and turned to face her, taking in the blue eyes, the face of a woman who was so gorgeous that he could see how he'd have wanted to pick her up. Yes, definitely his type, but the silence he was getting now from her was unnerving. "I guess I'm still confused and thrown as to what happened. We haven't even had a chance to talk. I mean, where did we meet? I don't remember you, and that's a shame, because you're gorgeous. All I can say in my defense is that I evidently drank so much that everything is a fog. You say you're a teacher, but last I remember was being at a gentlemen's club, and…"

"You mean a strip club? Yes, I know. You told me as you joined me at the bar," she said. When he blinked, she reached over and rested a hand on his leg. "Not at the strip club. I'm not a stripper. At Circus Circus, you bought a round for us, tequila. Then you suggested the Omni, and we cabbed it over and had more drinks. We ordered food, and you drank more." She pulled her hand away, and he had to look down at where it had been on his knee. He couldn't even remember her touch, and that was something he didn't forget with women. This was the first time he could remember ever drinking so much he couldn't remember. He wondered if his dad was likely to have a sit-down with him about this next.

"And how did we end up getting married?" he asked, and he didn't need to look over to his dad to know he likely wanted to know the same thing.

Angie sat up straighter, and he could see the tension turning into anger as she narrowed her eyes, glancing from him to his dad. "Oh, I see what this is," she said. She actually stood up and laughed, not from happiness but from hurt, he thought. The only thing he was sure about was that he could feel the hair on the back of his neck standing up, a warning that he was pushing the wrong way.

"Uh, I'm not sure what you're thinking…" He stopped talking when she flicked all her blue pissed-off gaze onto him, and he couldn't help thinking she was ready to slug him.

"You mean you and your father aren't under the

impression that I somehow arranged all this, the marriage? Oh, yeah, and I dumped all that booze down your throat? It was your signature on the marriage certificate, and it was your idea to get married. Yes, even I still can't believe what I did, but you were charming, Michael. We both drank way too much, but it was you, all you." She pointed to him, leaning over, and he caught an eyeful of her cleavage. "It was you who joked about all the wedding chapels, the drive-in weddings. Next thing I knew, you had us in the cab and talked the cabbie into driving to the first chapel. You paid for the package, and then we were standing in front of a lady in an angel costume, who was slipping a ring on my finger, and then we were back in the cab and off to the MGM, and you want to know what happened next?"

"What do you want?" Neil interrupted with quiet calm that masked his anger. He hated games, and Michael knew his dad wasn't going to give an inch here even though he was still trying to wrap his head around what she'd said. It had been him, all him? There was no way. So why the hell couldn't he remember?

"Excuse me?" she said. It didn't take a genius to see that she wasn't going to make this easy.

"I asked what you want to sign the annulment and admit to this mistake, and then you both walk away." Neil spoke so directly, and he didn't miss the punch in his words.

She said nothing as she pulled in a breath and opened her mouth to speak, then just shook her head and lifted her hands in surrender. She took a step back the minute she understood his dad's meaning, and instead of saying anything, she walked out of the room.

He looked over to his dad, and he could see even Neil didn't know what to make of it. Then she appeared in the doorway, a gold purse over her shoulder.

"You know what?" she said. "I'm hungry. I haven't eaten since this morning, so I'm going to go out and get something. You two…" She lifted her hand when he went to stand. "Stay or go." She shrugged, then stepped back, opened the door, and walked out.

Chapter Nine

"Angie, wait."

She kept walking and didn't look his way as he jogged up beside her, her heels clicking under the street lights. She could still feel the outrage pulsing through her blood. She was past furious, and though she was fighting the urge to cry, she knew damn well that was a mistake she couldn't make, considering the time she'd taken to get her makeup just right. Black smudges wouldn't get her free appies and drinks.

His hand slid around her elbow, and he pulled her back, holding her.

"Hey, seriously?" she snapped, but he didn't let go. In fact, he stood there, looking down at her, his dark brown eyes catching the light, and that just added to the package. What was wrong with her? It wasn't as if she hadn't been with a good-looking guy before, but there was something about Michael and his chemistry and this attraction. Even sober, it had her wanting to do something really stupid, like slide her hands up his arms and offer her lips to him to kiss again. How could he not remember?

"I can see you're angry. My dad has a way about him… He always gets right to business. He didn't exactly handle it tactfully," he added, and she just stared at him as he slowly let his hand fall away. Her arm mourned the touch, and she'd noticed the missing ring. Maybe it hadn't been a brilliant idea on her part to slip it on. It had been a whim that she really didn't want to analyze that closely.

"Why exactly is your dad here, anyway? I mean, you're a grown man, yet you have your dad here to fix this? To, what, buy me out, handle me, and make me go away?" Yup, the anger was pumping through her body again, and she looked up the street, not really seeing but knowing that there were people on the street, cars driving by.

"Point taken," he said. "I never really considered it that way. My dad is a man who doesn't take no for an answer. I humored him, but I have no intention of letting him handle this. Sorry about that, but we do need to talk and take care of it."

She just took him in, sad but aware that he saw all this as a mistake, a giant one. She couldn't help the ache that filled her chest even though she knew it wasn't rational. What was wrong with her? It had to be all the stress she was under. Her stomach rumbled again loudly, and she could feel the edges of hunger really gnaw at her stomach. That was another reason she was likely not about to see reason.

"Look, I need to get something to eat, so…" She gestured with her thumb up the street.

"Okay, dinner it is. So what's good?" he said and started walking, and he actually held out his arm so she could slip her hand over it and follow him. It was a gentlemanly move she hadn't expected.

"At Caesars, you can usually get shrimp cocktails for under a dollar," she said. Then there were the appies she could sometimes snag and the food people left beside the slots. Yes, she'd resorted to helping herself to someone's half-eaten nachos, but that wasn't something she was about to share. Hungry was hungry, and finding ways to eat for nothing was becoming her way of life.

Michael stopped walking and turned to look down at her. "I thought you were hungry," he said. "Listen, why don't I take you out for a real dinner? Name it."

Just hearing him say that had her mouth watering. "Italian? I would love some pasta, fettucine, veal," she said, then glanced up the street to where her place was, and he could feel the way he was watching her. He likely had more questions, but at this point, if she didn't eat something soon, she was going to be in real trouble. She could feel how shaky she was getting, and she never liked to push her hunger to this point.

"Italian it is, but let me just tell my dad," he said. "Leaving him at your place alone…"

Right, not a great idea. "So he'll be joining us, then," she said. Could she sit across the table from him at this point? Yes, because she was so damn hungry she didn't care who it was she'd have to sit with.

"No, it'll be just us. Dinner, and we'll talk, but I'll take the car, and my dad…well, he can occupy himself on the strip." Michael had her turned and walking back to her condo, up the steps, and he even opened the front door for her. She stepped in, and he followed, closing the door.

"Dad?" Michael called out, and he settled his hand on the small of her back as they stepped into the living room.

She froze as she saw the hard lines of Neil's face as he held up her eviction papers. He was reading them. She was horrified and hurt. She was sure she'd tucked them into a pile of bills on the corner of the kitchen counter, with an empty fruit bowl over them.

"So what's this?" Neil asked and held them out, and Michael reached around and took the notice from his dad. She didn't have to look his way to see the shock on his face. She was horrified, embarrassed, and furious for being so stupid to walk out the door and leave Neil in her place.

"They're eviction papers. I'm sure you can see that. I have to leave in two days," she said matter of factly, mainly because she didn't know what else to say.

"Why do you need to move?" Michael asked, looking over her head and around. "This looks like a nice place, from what I can see."

She shrugged and slipped the gold purse off her shoulder, clutching it with both hands, mainly to do something to occupy herself. She took in his dad, who was still staring at her as if she had an agenda, then Michael, who looked confused. He wasn't about to get involved and would likely be out the door in less than thirty seconds.

"I can't afford the rent, the increase…" She gestured to the paper. "Pretty self-explanatory." She could feel her hands shaking, and she was hit with a wave of dizziness. There was a hand on her arm as the room started spinning. "I don't feel well…" she thought she said, and then everything went black.

Chapter Ten

____

S he fainted.

Michael caught her before she hit the floor. He lifted her in his arms and was stunned at how light she was before he rested her on the sofa, her head on the cushion. "Should we call an ambulance?" he said to his dad, who pulled back the sofa table. She started to stir a few seconds later.

"Give her a second. Looks like she's coming around," Neil said.

She lifted her hand and moved her head from side to side, blinking her eyes open, and he took in the confusion as he leaned over her.

"What happened?" she said, but he saw the moment the confusion left, and she moved to sit up.

"No, just stay down there. You fainted. One minute we were talking, and the next you went down. If I hadn't caught you, you would have been on the floor. Are you all right? We should take you to the hospital."

She turned, looking up at his dad, who'd moved closer beside him. He could see how awkward she felt. "No, no...

no hospital. I'm fine. I'm just hungry, is all. Likely my blood sugar is low."

Neil walked into the kitchen as Angie pushed herself up to sit. Her skirt had already ridden up indecently, and Michael helped her up, letting his hands run over her bare arms, her skin.

"There's no food in here other than stale crackers and a jar of pickles with, like, one pickle," Neil said. He opened the box of crackers and paused before he reached in and pulled out a pearl necklace. "You have a necklace in a cracker box?"

Angie's odd expression was more annoyed than anything. "My mother's pearls. She left them to me. They're worth something." She shrugged as she ran a hand over the back of her neck. "It's the perfect place to hide them. Who's going to think to look in a cracker box?"

She sounded so reasonable, and he didn't know what to say as his dad stuffed the pearls back in the box and rested it on the counter.

"So, food," Michael said. "You need food, and there's nothing here. We were going for dinner, but maybe that's not going to work. You need to eat now, so let's order some food, and, Dad, maybe you could pick it up?"

Neil was already thumbing through his phone, and Angie just nodded.

"Ah, Italian," Michael said. "Veal, fettucine…" He took in the surprise in Angie's expression.

"You remembered," she said. He was positive he saw the beginning of a smile. He needed to have a conversation with her, but not with his dad here. He could hear him on the phone now, ordering what sounded like a lot of food.

"Okay, about fifteen minutes," Neil said. "A place not far from here, by the looks of it, so I'll pick up the food." He slid his cell phone in the back pocket of his blue jeans, and Michael thought of how Angie might see him: Neil was dressed as he always was, smart but casual, ready for business. His dress shirt was deep blue, with the sleeves rolled up, his gold Rolex flashing. The diamond in his ear made such a contrast.

"Michael, can I have a word?" Neil said and gestured from where he was leaning against the island in the kitchen. Angie slid her feet to the floor and pulled at the edges of her skirt, and Michael joined his dad, wondering what he wanted to say now. It would likely be a warning of some kind, as if he didn't have a clue how to think for himself.

"What?" Michael said. He didn't miss the way his dad crossed his arms as he approached and seemed to settle his stance.

Neil tilted his chin behind him to Angie. "I'll get the food, but I'm wondering about the wisdom of leaving you alone with her."

He had to fight the urge to roll his eyes. "Seriously?" was all he said, then shook his head. "No, I'm staying. Besides, it would be better if I talk to her. The way you're coming across, it feels as if you're trying to break her. She's not a business deal, Dad, and right now, she's hungry and about to lose her home, from the looks of it. Go get the food."

Neil hesitated before nodding and rested his hand on his shoulder. "Just make sure you talk and that's all," he said, the edge in his voice sounding like a warning, before he pulled out the keys to the new Lincoln he had rented at the airport and started to the door. "I'll be back in less than half an hour."

Neil looked back just once before pulling it open and leaving, and as the door closed, there was a moment of silence. Michael swore he could hear a clock ticking from somewhere in the condo.

"Okay, so let's talk," he said.

Angie lifted a pillow onto her lap, against her stomach, and said nothing as she lifted her gaze to him. He could see the vulnerability she'd likely been trying to hide and took in the eviction notice his dad had left on the island. He thought about the lack of food and looked back over to the hot babe. The way she was dressed didn't paint a flattering picture.

"You want to tell me what's really going on?" he added.

She glanced away as if needing to gather her thoughts. "You may want to be more specific, Michael…" she started.

He lifted the notice and held it up, then gestured to the kitchen behind him before settling the paper down, not missing the rent she was paying. He blinked, because it was a ridiculous amount.

She sighed. "I see you want to know if I did something," she said. He wasn't sure what he was seeing: a woman so complex, a woman who was a virtual stranger.

"Did you? I'm not sure why you would rent a place for that amount. I mean, how much can you make as a kindergarten teacher?" Maybe she was just one of those people who lived beyond her means.

She pulled in a breath. "It didn't start out that way. It was reasonable when I rented this place, and no, kindergarten teachers are not paid a lot, especially when you add in my student loans. The new owners who purchased the condo have raised my rent three times, basically tripling it. If you're about to say I should just move, that would be easier said than done, considering I basically have only a couple of days to come up with another place. Should I have just left the first time they doubled my rent? Yes, likely. Maybe I would've been able to scrape enough together to come up with what I need to rent another place, but I didn't, so here I am," she said so matter of factly, then moved the pillow beside her on the sofa and unzipped her boots before pulling them off and dumping them on the floor. "Is this my fault? Yeah, in a manner of speaking, but I didn't expect to have the rug yanked out from under me…" She gestured help-lessly and stood, a little shaky. When he took a step to her, she lifted her hand. "I'm fine, just getting a glass of water."

"I'll get it for you. Sit down," he said, and she did.

"Thank you. Glasses are in the cupboard by the sink," she said.

He opened the cupboard and pulled out a glass, then turned on the tap to fill it with water and walked it back over to her. Her blue eyes flicked up to him, and she hesi-tated before taking it. He sat down on the sofa beside her as she drank, allowing his eyes to take her in again. She was slim, sexy, but he wondered if in fact she was a little too slim.

"So you're being evicted because you can't pay the rent, and you have no food in your house because, I assume, you can't afford to eat," he added.

She gave everything she had to that glass of water. "Basically," she finally said, then looked his way.

"But you were going out? The way you're dressed—"

She let out a breath that sounded frustrated. "Don't forget that when we met, you loved what you saw, and you didn't hesitate to let me know, to touch, to kiss, to have any and all of me. Michael, drunk or not, you zeroed in on me, and you did everything every guy does. You saw a pretty face, a sexy body, and everything I wore accentuated that, from the clothes, to the makeup, to the boots. You guys are all about the looks."

He felt as though he'd just had his hand slapped and been called out, because that was exactly what he'd done. He wanted a woman who was hot and sexy, and she'd just spelled it all out for him.

She slid around and leaned forward. Her lips, her cleavage—he could see everything and wanted nothing more than to lean in and take what she was offering when he heard the door open.

"Food's here," Neil said. "Busy place, too, but it smells great…"

It was like an icy splash of water, but his dad's interruption was welcome. Angie got up and strode barefoot to the kitchen while he did his best to pull it together.

"Michael, didn't you hear me?" Neil said.

Michael pressed his hands to his knees and gave his head a shake, looking over to Angie, who was seated on a bar stool at the island with a carton of fettucine, shoving a forkful in her mouth.

His dad just glanced to Angie and then over to him. "I ordered extra, a linguine Portofino, your favorite, and cala-mari, salad…"

Neil really had outdone himself. As Michael took in Angie, who was now eating and focusing everything on that pasta, he couldn't help wondering what he'd have done if his dad hadn't walked in when he had.

"I'm good," Michael said as he sat back on the sofa and tried to rack his brain, to remember his birthday and meeting Angie, whether it had happened as she said. He didn't know why, but he was suddenly struck by the fear that there might be a lot more to the story than she was saying, and a whole lot more holes that needed to be filled in.

Chapter Eleven

"I'll give you three hundred for the set."

Angie stared at the guy in her living room, who was shuffling his stance from side to side, dressed as if he'd just come from a construction jobsite. His buddy was outside with their pickup, smoking a cigarette. Colin, he'd said his name was. He was the only one to answer the ad she'd posted online the night before to sell her living room sofa, chair, and tables.

"But it's only a year old, and I paid just over fifteen hundred..." she started, but he shook his head, and she knew she'd have to take it. Considering the cost of moving, she couldn't rent a larger storage unit and store everything for...how long? Her desperation must have been written all over her. She needed to move tomorrow, and she was dressed in her old jeans and a faded T-shirt, her hair pulled back in a ponytail. She didn't have a stitch of makeup on.

"Fine, I'll take it," she said as she watched him pull a wad of cash from his pocket and count out three hundred in fifties. He handed her the cash, and she stepped back while he lifted the chair and started outside with it. Colin and his buddy made short order of emptying her living room, minus the boxes she'd already packed, filled with photos and trinkets she couldn't and wouldn't sell, and the kitchen island, which held four open boxes now stuffed with her dishes, glasses, and pots and pans.

That left her bed, now just a mattress on the floor that no one wanted. The frame and dresser had sold earlier that day for two hundred and fifty, a steal, and had been picked up just before the living room set. At least now she had the extra cash to store everything, and the movers could bring the small truck tomorrow to pick up all the boxes and drop them off in storage locker 36C, which she'd rented for the month, hoping she'd find something, anything, long before that.

As of the next night, she'd be renting an Airbnb, a one bedroom with a shared bath in a condo, so at least she wouldn't be on the streets—not that she had any idea what to do and how to live on the streets. Thankfully, she wasn't completely without money. It was just that the ability to afford to live in this city was suddenly out of reach. What had happened to the rental market? It seemed as if when one unit disappeared, two Airbnb rentals popped up.

She'd beaten herself up over the situation for too long, though. Right now she needed to focus on a plan, on what she could do to fix her situation instead of wallowing in her woes and what could've and should've been.

Then there was Michael.

She was still embarrassed and…"raw" was the only word she could think of. She felt as if every nuance of who she was had been put under a microscope by his father the night before. She had felt cheap and worthless, but at least she'd eaten—and well, too. Although Michael hadn't said a word to her after his father returned with the food, she'd eaten and packaged up all the extras. They'd left with Neil saying, "Let us know where you get settled, because we still need to take care of this matter, which is of some importance," and that had been it.

She took in the gold band she was wearing, wondering whether it was worth anything. Likely not. She just had her mother's pearls, which were the only thing she had left of Hildy Debois and which she was not about to part with.

"You know what?" she said to herself. "At least you have dinner tonight, you have a job to go to on Monday, and maybe it's time to look at a roommate situation for now."

She slid the ring back on her finger, wanting to feel better because at least she had a job, a pay check on its way, but she was stuck in the cycle of living paycheck to paycheck and never getting ahead. She just needed a break, to find a landlord who wouldn't demand months of deposits on top of a ridiculous rent. Seriously, there had to be someone left who still believed in being a decent human and not taking advantage just because they could.

There was a knock on her door, and she hesitated a second, because she wasn't expecting anyone. The way her luck was going, it would likely be just someone else with more bad news.

She pulled open the door and took in Erin, the principal at her school, who had short brown hair and was dressed neat and tidy in light capris and a deep blue shirt.

"This is a surprise," Angie said, wondering why her boss would be standing at her front door.

"Sorry to barge in on you, Angie, but I wanted to have a talk with you about a complaint that was filed."

What was it about living in stress that seemed to create a constant roller coaster of emotions? A chill raced up her spine.

"Can I come in?" Erin asked, and at least that was enough to snap her out of it.

"Yes, yes, of course, come in," she said and gestured behind her, then took her time closing the door.

Erin stood in her now empty living room, looking around with a frown. "You're moving?" she said, though it wasn't really a question, as the boxes and empty room said everything.

Her stomach sank another notch. *No, I'm being evicted because I can't afford the outrageous rent.* "Yes, sorry, just in the middle of it." She forced a smile to her lips, one that wasn't returned. "You said there's a complaint…not about me?" She pressed her hand to her chest, feeling how fast her heart was pounding, glad she was dressed the way she was: respectable.

Erin lifted her hands and dramatically shut her eyes as she shook her head. "I'm sorry. Even I couldn't believe it, but the father of one of your kindergarten students came to me with concerns about your extracurricular activities."

She wasn't sure what expression was on her face as her jaw slackened and she stared at Erin, wondering what had been said. "Uh, about…?" she started.

Awkwardness spilled over Erin's face. "I'm just going to say this outright, because I'm still having a hard time wrapping my head around it. The father indicated you've been spotted frequenting many of the Vegas hotels, being solicited for sex, picking up men. I wouldn't have believed it, but one of the teachers mentioned something a while back about seeing you at the clubs and wondered if you were an escort on the side. Two times hearing it, and, well, there has to be something to it, right?"

Had the floor just moved? She thought it had. She stared at Erin and realized she was serious. She sputtered, "No! Oh my God, who would say something like that? I'm not a prostitute. What teacher said that, and who is this parent? That's a damn lie…" She pressed her hands to her face for a second, because this was just too much.

"Is that a wedding ring?"

She pulled her hands away from her face and realized Erin had spotted the wedding band she was still wearing. She stared at her hands and the cheap gold band on her finger. "Ah, yes it is."

"When did you get married? I didn't realize…" Erin actually glanced over her shoulder into the kitchen, likely looking around for her missing husband, whom she wouldn't find, because he wasn't real.

"Just recently. So the father who filed the complaint about me, who is he? And the teacher who said they saw me…" She crossed her arms, feeling the ring on her finger, and she couldn't explain why she felt as if it were some protection from whatever accusation this was.

"I'm not at liberty to disclose the parent, but he's a man with means. So you weren't frequenting the hotels, escorting?" Erin added, as if maybe this time she believed her.

Yes, she'd been at the hotels, bars, clubs, everywhere. "No, I'm not a hooker," she stated through gritted teeth.

"Well, it's possible someone else was mistaken for you. They do say everyone has a twin, and apparently yours is an escort. Is your husband around? It would be nice to meet him."

"No, he's not here right now—and you didn't tell me which teacher said they saw me," she added and crossed her arms over her chest, gripping them so tight she could feel the pull in her back. She took in the hesitation and wondered for a second whether Erin was going to refuse to tell her.

She sighed and said, "Roger Copeland."

Angie knew she was frowning and wondered if her disapproval showed. She hoped so, since Roger was known for his propensity to hit the slots, the tables, which was what had ended his first and second marriages. He had even gone bankrupt not once but twice, or so said the rumor mill. Even his four kids from both marriages wouldn't talk to him. She was at a loss.

"So my character is in question because of Roger, who is a walking moral compass, yet everyone is turning a blind eye to his gambling addiction?" She could feel her stress and worry from seconds ago turning to anger.

"If it were just Roger, of course not," Erin said, "but this parent has clout and isn't the kind of person I can brush off. He insists you be let go. His son is in your class, and he doesn't want a teacher who's a part-time hooker, as he called it, anywhere near his kid. He was quite adamant. He's threatened to go to the board, and… Look, this is ridiculous, I agree, but maybe if your husband and you come in, I'll arrange a meeting so the father understands his mistake, and we can put these allegations to bed. He must have mistaken someone else for you. It's a simple case of mistaken identity. We'll prove it."

She didn't say anything for a second. "You know what? Just tell this parent you don't need us there." She was stuck on how suddenly Erin had shifted to being on her side now that she had a ring on her finger, and her anger returned. What did being married have to do with suddenly not being guilty of what she was accused of?

Erin was shaking her head. "The only problem is, and it's kind of a headache, this man insists it's you. Unfortunately, I think he won't believe me. Me saying he's wrong isn't going to fly, so let's just shut this down before he talks to anyone else or does take it to the board. Is your husband here?" She glanced over her shoulder again.

"No, he's not. He's…out of town," she added, and she didn't miss the way Erin suddenly appeared suspicious. "He's at a game. He's a hockey player, Michael Friessen."

There it was. She'd once again been deemed respectable. Yes, her husband was a hockey star, a right wing as a rookie, but he was on his way to the pros. She'd known who he was even before he told her all about the Canucks' offer, his future, and the money he would be making. He was arrogant, hot, sexy, and so damn good looking—a star athlete that women everywhere wanted.

"A public figure? Even better," Erin said. "Now I have to meet him. You being his wife will definitely go a long way to shutting down all of these ridiculous accusations."

All Angie could do was stare at the woman who had the power to end her career in a second. What she was asking was absolutely impossible. If Erin ever learned what really happened, how she and Michael had really met, how they'd made their way to a Vegas strip chapel, drunk, how she'd married a stranger she'd known for a few hours… well, her credibility would be destroyed. Then this accusation of her being a hooker would actually have merit, even though, out of everything she had done, that was the one thing that wasn't true.

———————

Chapter Twelve

He tossed his hockey bag in the corner of the hotel room and knocked over the luggage rack. After today, he'd be relocating to join his new team in Vancouver. The contract had come down the pipe that morning for one year, with no starting bonus, but still. The quarter mill starting salary was nothing to sneeze at, and as he stared at the numbers on the paper, he knew that was far different from the salary Angie made. Being a teacher didn't get you wealthy.

"Whoa, seriously, chill out. What's up with you?" Kyle said from where he was lounging on one of the two queen beds, pillows propped behind him, his hair wet, dressed in sweats and barefoot, thumbing across the screen of his cell phone.

What could he say? He was seriously pissed at everything about his situation. "I left her there," he snapped. "We just up and walked out last night, had a plane to catch, and I left her. Christ, I don't even know what to say. She's being evicted, she had no food in her place, and we're still married."

He knew he was ranting, but he was furious over the fact that he was married because of some drunken, idiotic decision. More and more, he was convinced there had to be way more to the story than what she'd said, because her version put everything on him, and Michael Friessen couldn't be the kind of guy who would do something so careless.

Maybe that was why he was in such a crappy mood, because he didn't want to be responsible for any of this. When he drank with the boys, they were known for letting loose and really going to town, doing things they laughed about later, living the lives of carefree single guys, just having fun—except this time he was facing the consequences for something he couldn't remember.

Kyle just stared at him and then lifted his hand to sweep back his wet hair. "What did your dad say?"

"Who cares what my dad said? Fuck, Kyle, this is me, and I'm not some snot-nosed kid who needs daddy to run in and clean up my mess." That was also likely why he was as pissed as he was, because that was basically what had happened. He hadn't told his dad no and instead had let him insist on coming along, on handling something that was his mess. He wasn't proud, but he still needed to get to the bottom of exactly who had done what, and his dad having any part of it wasn't okay.

Kyle just stared at him with a "cut the bullshit" expression. "I've never heard you talk about your dad like that. If I were you, I'd let him handle this. You have bigger, more important things to focus on, like making sure you don't blow your shot at the big times."

He shrugged. "Dad mentioned hiring a private detective to do some digging, find out what's what." Then he would sit down with Angie and the annulment papers, hand her a check, get her to sign and go away. What had he said? Oh, yeah, that they would know her every secret and find out what had happened that night. A detective would talk to all the waitstaff, the bartenders, and anyone else who had seen them and would dig up the real story. People did love to talk.

He understood his dad's need to have all the facts and have the upper hand before they went in. He got it, he understood it, but something bothered him about the entire scenario after seeing Angie and her empty kitchen.

"Good idea," Kyle said. "Your dad's a smart man. Listen to him. Besides, you're in the big times now. Get your head together. Ditch the broad, meet a nice girl…"

Michael had stopped listening, knowing Kyle was still talking about a woman he didn't know, had never met. Everyone just assumed she wasn't a nice girl.

"You know she passed out?" Michael slid out the desk chair and sat down.

"What do you mean, passed out?" Kyle pulled his feet up and gestured to him.

"She was hungry, said she hadn't eaten, but I think the confrontation with my dad had something to do with it. You know how my dad is, barging in and demanding to end this farce of a marriage. He's pretty direct and put the blame on her. Even I picked up that much. She was rattled, upset… Not that I know shit, but still—and crap, there was this eviction notice. She's about to lose her place. She can't afford the rent, and we just left. I should have given her some money…something. I should call her. I don't know, but I'm bothered by the way we left."

Kyle was still staring at him with that arrogant hard look he always had. "You know shit about her. For all you know, she's playing you. I can see she's managed to worm her way in, get you thinking you're responsible for her. This is where a woman can take you for everything. Don't do it, man. Let your dad dig up everything and send her a check and be on your way. You don't have any idea what she wants, and for all you know, she could be working some angle." He was standing now and strode over to the dresser, yanked out a T-shirt, and pulled it over his head.

"You mean the starving and about to be homeless angle?" Michael snapped.

Kyle shot him a look. "You said she's a teacher, but don't forget who you are. You know well enough the number of babes out there wanting to hook up with you. Let your dad check out her story. If she's about to be on the streets, that should tell you there's likely a lot about her that you don't want to know. Maybe she has trouble following her—maybe she is trouble. Maybe she did something, and that's not your problem."

Kyle could be a real dick at times.

"Whatever it is, don't go there," he continued, "because I know that look. You're getting sucked in." Kyle jabbed his finger into Michael's chest and pressed. "You're a pretty boy, and you know it. We all know it. You have a soft spot for the ladies. You got yourself buried so deep into shit that I can see you're getting sucked in, so do yourself a favor and just walk away. Toss the chick some cash, and then cut your losses, but don't go any further down the road of thinking you have some responsibility or owe her anything in any way. You don't!" Kyle jabbed his finger again into his chest and then stepped back. As he glanced in the mirror at his image, he flexed the muscles in his forearms.

"I'm not getting sucked in," Michael said, "but I'm a living, breathing human, and I'm not a dick. I may not be responsible for her troubles, but nonetheless, she's in trouble, and if there's something I can do to help her, find a place, something, anything, then that would be the right thing to do. Then when we part ways, at least I won't be thinking I've just kicked her to the curb. Because right now, that's exactly how I feel."

"Don't do it." Kyle didn't look his way as he ran his fingers through his hair and then reached in the drawer to pull out a pair of socks. "You're leaving tonight. Pack your stuff, get on the plane, and don't look back. You've got a shot very few get. I know I would kill for what you have, but this is a distraction. She's a distraction, and you can't afford to have distractions right now because it will mess with your game. Although the NHL appears to be all glam and fun, you know very well what you've been doing is to get ready for that shot. It's a commitment, an enormous one, and the life you're now stepping into is going to have demands you don't have now."

He heard what his friend was saying, but at the same time, what was eating at him was the fact that while he was here, following his dream, there were two very big facts he couldn't shake. Even though he didn't know a thing about Angie, he was married to her, and she was in trouble.

Chapter Thirteen

His dad couldn't help himself, of course. Michael had grown up with a father who always needed to stick his nose into the lives of him and his sister, Cat. His mom's life, too. Neil handled everything, so finding out that his dad had purchased a condo for him in Vancouver shouldn't have been a surprise.

When he stepped into the fairly new three-bedroom, three-bathroom open concept condo, which had already been furnished, he thought it was unnecessary, but his dad was still waiting for a "Thanks, Dad, this is great." He hadn't provided it, mainly because Angie had yet to return the last three messages he'd left on his second night in a new city.

Yes, he was worried.

The life of an NHL player came with an unbelievably demanding schedule, and he was still coming to grips with having been thrown in at the deep end.

"Michael, grab some plates, would you? The lasagna's ready," Neil said. He was actually wearing an apron over his dark dress pants and black lightweight knit. Candy was chopping up a salad at the island with a glass of white wine beside her, and he was aware that the guest suite in his condo was as spacious and comfortable as the master. He figured his parents were planning to visit often. Then again, his father had bought the place, which really made it his, not Michael's. He wanted to point out to his dad that he was the guest, not the other way around, but he was still thinking about how to find a way to go and see Angie.

"So you've said not more than two words since you got home from the arena," Candy added as Michael opened cupboards to find the plates that he hadn't bought.

"What do you want me to say?" He couldn't believe the schedule. Aside from game days, they skated twice, and there were no days off. Tomorrow, the team would be on a charter to Boston. The life he'd dreamed of having, he was now living. It was everything he'd always wanted, except for the fact that right now, he couldn't enjoy any of it.

"How about what's going on with you?" Neil said. "You spent your whole life getting ready for this. You dreamed of hockey as a kid, lived it, breathed it. All those early mornings, hotels, travelling, pulled muscles, and not giving in, and here you are, moping around as if someone kicked your puppy. This isn't still about the girl?" He rested the steaming casserole on a hotplate on the round oak table for four. Michael set the plates down along with knives and forks he'd grabbed from a drawer, and his mom followed, putting the salad on the table along with two bottles of dressing.

He pulled out one of the oak chairs and sat down, then scooped up lasagna and dumped it on his plate. His mom sat across from him, and he didn't bother looking her way as he dished up salad and dumped the creamy dressing on it. "This is my dream job," he said. "It's great. This has nothing to do with being a hockey pro, but the fact is that I can't get a hold of Angie. I left messages that she hasn't returned, either. So yes, it's about the girl. I'm worried, considering the state we left her in. It wasn't right," he snapped.

His mom slid her gaze over to his dad, who finally took a seat. Neil shook his head, likely ready to get into it. He was never a man to back down, but then, neither was Michael. Evidently, that was where he'd gotten his stubbornness from.

"I hired a private detective to start digging," Neil said. "Wasn't going to get into this now, but he emailed me a preliminary report of what he's found."

Candy was still staring at his dad, who was scooping up some lasagna and salad, before she slid her gaze over to him. "You know, Neil," she said, "I understand your need to handle everything. It's been a source of contention between us. I love you, but Michael is an adult, and there's a point where he's going to have to handle some of this himself."

"Thanks, Mom. That's exactly what I've been saying." He jabbed his fork in the air toward his mom, noting her pissed-off expression as she leveled her gaze his way.

"Really? Because it doesn't seem that way, from where I'm sitting. You said you've called her, but why? To settle this and fix this mistake of a marriage that shouldn't have happened? You think I don't know how rowdy you and your friends are? The booze, the parties, the girls… You may not have thought there would be consequences, Michael, but there always are. So what is it that you want, to make her go away?" His mom took a small square of lasagna and cut into it, blowing off the steam before she took a bite.

"I've called her because I don't like how it was left in Vegas. I'm sure Dad filled you in on how down and out she was. What did we do but order takeout, feed her, and leave…?"

"You have a career in the pros," Neil said. "You've signed a contract with the Canucks, and now you're living in a new city. You're very much right about one thing: You have a very demanding schedule. For eight months of the year, you'll have no days off, no weekends, and no vacations. You're in the big leagues now, either traveling or on the ice every day. There was no option of staying, of doing something. All that can be done right now is to find out everything about Angie Debois.

"She really doesn't have much going for her," Neil continued. "My lawyers have already crafted the annulment, and we'll cut her a check. It will be a nice little payday for her. She'll be able to afford a modest roof over her head, feed herself, get her life together. Then you don't need to spend one more minute worrying or thinking you owe her anything. Get her out of your mind, because you don't have time for that kind of distraction." Neil took in Michael and Candy. "And your mom and I aren't here to babysit you. Your life is here now. We're leaving in the morning to go home. We'll be back for your home game in two weeks, and by then the girl will be handled. Candy, he's a big boy, but in this, he's over his head."

Michael paused with his fork midway to his mouth and looked over to his dad. This was that shrewd all-business side of him that he had admired and tried to emulate at times, but right now it seemed as if his dad was trying to handle his life.

"Over my head, seriously?" he said. "No, Dad, this is my problem, and I'm a grown adult. I don't need you to step in and fix this. This is my mess, my situation. I'm the one who got drunk and screwed up and ended up married to a stranger, so I'll be the one to fix it, but first I need to make sure she's okay. I'll sit her down and get her to sign papers, but as for cutting her a check to, what, pay her off…?" He just shook his head, because he didn't think he had the stomach to let that happen. "If anyone is going to pay her anything, it's going to be me." He set his fork down and pushed back his chair, then stood up, taking in the way his mom and dad watched him.

"And in case I didn't say it, Dad, thanks for the condo, but I can't accept this. This is your place. You bought it. So the next free day I have, I'll find my own place." *A much smaller place*, he thought. "Now, if you'll excuse me, I'm going to try Angie again, and then I'll make a plan on how to fix this mess myself." He started around the table.

"Michael," his dad called out and looked back to him. "I'll send you the investigator's report. Have a look at it before you call."

He didn't know what to make of the comment. Knowing his dad, there was something in there that he wasn't going to want to see.

Chapter Fourteen

"Angie, do you have a second?" Erin tapped on the open door of the kindergarten classroom where she had eighteen boys and girls sitting cross legged on the floor while she read them *The One Day House.*

"I'm just in the middle of story time, so…" Angie said, but she took in the way Erin gestured outside. Her expression said she wasn't going to wait. At the same time, Melinda Cravett, one of the support workers, strode in.

"I can finish for you until you get back," Melinda said in a low voice. She reached for the book as Angie stood up from the child's chair she was sitting on. Her knee-length brown and white skirt brushed her bare legs as she strode in flat sandals to the door, where she saw a man—tall, with a round face and dark hair, soft in the middle, dressed in dark pants and a light dress shirt. He appeared distinguished and handsome.

"Angie, this is Mr. Hasek," Erin said. "He's the father of Jason Hasek, one of your students."

Angie held out her hand even though alarm shot through her. This had to be the father who wanted her fired. He had seen her at one of the hotels, but she didn't remember seeing him. She was sure he wasn't one of the many men who'd bought her drinks or dinner with the hope of something more.

He shook her hand, but it was out of obligation. There wasn't a smile or any of the social ease that was usually offered when people met for the first time.

"Okay, and…" Angie started.

"Let's take this to my office," Erin interrupted, and they started around the corner.

No one said anything as they entered the office, where Erin shut the door and gestured to one of the chairs opposite her desk. Angie strode to it and sat down. A few strands of hair had slipped from her single braid. She could feel the dampness under her arms and hoped it didn't show through her deep brown blouse.

"Angie, I spoke with you a few days ago about Mr. Hasek, who came to see me and indicated that—"

"I filed a complaint because you, my dear, shouldn't be teaching children," he said. "I told you before, Mrs. Brown, that either you see to it she's fired or I will go to the board."

Angie didn't pull her gaze from the man, taking in everything about him, from his icy blue eyes, to his dark hair with threads of gray. He was still standing by the door, his hands now on his hips. He wore a heavy gold ring on his ring finger, encrusted with diamonds, and a thick gold watch. She did her best to try to remember meeting him. She couldn't place him, and that wasn't sitting well with her.

"I was telling Mr. Hasek that he had to be mistaken, and you and your husband would gladly meet with him," Erin continued. "Her husband is Michael Friessen. He plays for the Canucks."

Angie turned her head and narrowed her gaze, wondering how she knew that. She should have known and would have known if she hadn't been busy putting everything she had left into storage and sleeping at an overpriced Airbnb, which had turned out to be a room in a condo shared with an overweight guy who never left his easy chair. To make matters worse, the mattress was hard and the shower leaked. She crossed her legs and rested her hands over her bare knee, feeling her heart pounding. She knew she should say something.

The man gestured toward her, and it wasn't lost on her that she'd been reduced to *my dear*, though that was apparently better than the alternative he was accusing her of. "Impressive, I guess, if it were true," he said. "You're married to Michael Friessen? I wonder why you live here when he's in Vancouver. That's a long way from here, and it only opens up more questions."

"Well, I'm not really sure how it's any of your business who I'm married to," Angie said, "and really, what does this have to do with the issue at hand? From what I understand, you've accused me of something vile, and I take exception. I'm a great teacher, so let's just put aside your accusation, which I'm still having trouble wrapping my head around. Is there an issue with how I'm teaching my students, your son?" She didn't pull her gaze from the man, who was watching her in a way that seemed indecent. This was the first time she had ever wanted to slap someone.

"Whores cannot be schoolteachers," he said. "You may have convinced the principal it wasn't you, but just looking at you, I know it was. You're a beautiful woman, Miss Debois, but the minute you decided to prostitute yourself, you lost the right to teach. You have no business being here, and I was clear with you, Mrs. Brown, that you must fire her. If you don't, it will be your job as well that's in jeopardy. I've already put a call in to your board, and for the record, Miss Debois, this last Hail Mary of yours, throwing out the name of a hockey pro, is pitiful."

Just the way he spoke to her, she could feel such hate.

"Now, just a minute, Mr. Hasek," Erin said. "You can't just accuse Angie of lying. Angie, please just call your husband. We'll meet, and…"

"No, we can't meet, because Michael isn't here. You all know this. He's in Vancouver now and can't just show up because you want him to. Having him here is irrelevant. So if you meet him, what does that have to do with you accusing me of being a hooker?" she stated, taking in both Hasek and her boss. "Nothing, it has nothing to do with it, because I'm not. Having him suddenly come in and, what, vouch for me? Is that what we've become? Are we taking a step back forty years, as if being married suddenly makes you respectable? No." She shook her head, feeling a fire burn deep in her belly. "This is wrong, and you know it's wrong. You accuse me of being some prostitute? I want to know where you would even come up with something like that. This is a fabrication, a lie, a…"

He took a step toward her and rested one hand on the desk as he leaned down. "I know because my partner picked you up and bragged about his night. I know because I saw you at the MGM, at the bar with another guy, and my partner pointed you out—just a hot babe with mile-long legs, and he urged me to take you for a test drive. It didn't take me more than a minute to recognize you under all that makeup and what little you were wearing. You clean up well, Miss Debois, but you're not teaching my son."

He was so close, but then he stepped back, glancing once to Erin. "She doesn't set foot back in that classroom, or it will be your job I come for next," he said, then pulled the door open, his gaze hard and filled with warning. As he stepped out, he allowed his gaze to linger on Angie, starting from her toes and dragged all the way up over her breasts and to her eyes. It was indecent, letting her know how little he thought of her, as if she were nothing but a toy for men to play with. Then he was gone, and Erin rushed to the door and closed it.

"Okay, that didn't go well," she said. "I thought we agreed you'd call your husband. You are married, right?" she asked, but Angie was still stuck on the horror of what had gone down. "Well, I just don't know what to say, Angie. Until this can get straightened out, I'm going to have to ask you to take a leave of absence—indefinitely."

"He's lying," Angie said. "I'm not a prostitute. You're taking the word of a man who trusted his friend's bragging?" She realized her voice squeaked.

Erin looked at her helplessly as if her hands were tied. Angie knew when someone was walking away, when someone was done with her, and all she could think was that she'd just lost the only thing that she had left in her life, her job as a teacher.

Chapter Fifteen

He slammed his fist on the alarm until it finally stopped buzzing, knocking it on the floor. It took him a second to realize where he was. Right, at home in the new condo his dad had bought. He flicked on the bedside light and yawned, seeing it was seven a.m., enough time for a long hot shower and breakfast, and then he had to meet the trainers at nine sharp, then practice from ten thirty to lunch, and at two thirty there was the charter to Boston for the game the next night.

He was still trying to wrap his head around all the dirt his father's detective, Xander Jennings, had uncovered about Angie. There was nothing about what he read that was in any way flattering. Worse was the fact that it was Xander, his sister's long-time boyfriend, who'd had to dig it up. He hoped he hadn't shared any of it with Cat, but the fact that Xander knew anything at all about what was going on was yet another sore spot with him.

He stumbled from bed, stepping onto the cold hardwood, and flicked the switch on the bathroom wall for the in-floor heating. He took in the huge walk-in shower, the double sinks, and the soaker tub before he reached in and turned on the shower, letting it heat up as he took in his image in the mirror. He seemed to be in a perpetually pissed-off state as of late, and he yawned.

He'd stayed up way too late, because once he'd started reading the report his dad had forwarded him by email, he hadn't been able to stop. Angie Debois was twenty-four and had grown up in Madera, California, the daughter of Dirk and Hildy Debois, with a brother, Paddy, and a sister, Rae. Her father was an alcoholic who was on and off the wagon, and her mother had died when she was ten from small-cell lung cancer that had gone undiagnosed. Her father's main source of income was welfare.

At thirteen, Angie and her sister had been picked up for shoplifting nail polish and a pack of Marlboros. Two years later, they had been arrested with fake IDs in a bar for offering sex to an undercover officer for fifty bucks. They'd gone to juvie for a year, and two months later they had been picked up again as part of a gang defacing public property. Paddy had no arrests but was a high school drop-out and was, he suspected, currently following in his father's footsteps as a roughneck on an oil rig. Dirk lived in Mobile and was the manager of a welfare-run trailer park. Rae was divorcing her second husband, a used car sales-man, and had no kids. The entire history of this family let him know they didn't exchange Christmas cards or have each other's backs. It was depressing and left him with a lot more questions than answers, especially considering the part about Angie being a teacher was, in fact, true. How had she managed to pull that off after her fucked-up childhood?

Maybe that was why he hadn't called her a fourth time.

He stood with his hand on the wall, bracing himself as he let the hot spray run over him until it ran lukewarm. He toweled off, brushed his teeth, and took his time getting dressed in dress pants and a long-sleeved shirt. He packed his suit, the navy one, a tie, and his black polished dress shoes, everything he would need for the overnight, because he wouldn't be coming home after practice. Nope, airport, hotel, and of course a midnight curfew. Tomorrow would be more of the same, with a late lunch, seeing the trainer, visiting medical for injuries, getting a massage… Then there would be equipment checks and game night, followed by a midnight flight back home.

Somewhere in there, he needed to make sense of the woman he was married to, figure out a way to fix this mess, and get this annulment taken care of.

His dad was in the kitchen already when he made his way down and dumped his suitcase on the landing by the stairs. His equipment was already in the back of his sporty SUV, parked in the underground garage.

"Made you oatmeal, eggs, orange juice." Neil's hair was a mess, and he was drinking coffee, barefoot, in blue jeans and a faded T-shirt. His mom, evidently, was still asleep.

"Sounds great." Michael poured a coffee and pulled out the blender to dump some protein powder in. His dad already had the fridge open and handed him the carton of milk. Of course it was fully stocked. That was just what his dad did. "Thanks," he said and dumped milk into the blender, then flicked it on as his dad slid a plate of eggs in front of him at the island and a bowl filled with oatmeal.

"You know, Dad, I can feed myself. Although I appreciate this breakfast thing…" he started as he poured the protein shake in a glass his dad set on the island. He pulled out a stool and sat down after downing half the shake, then dug into the eggs, feeling his dad watching him. He took in his amber eyes, knowing he had something on his mind.

"You get a chance to read the detective's report?"

Michael reached for the OJ and downed the glass, then reached for the oatmeal, which had dates and nuts already on top. Yes, his dad was again seeing to it that he had the carbs, protein, and nutrition to fuel his body. He poured milk and considered what to say. "You mean the one you had Xander write up? I did. Is this where you want to insult my choice in women? And why Xander, seriously?" he snapped, then jabbed his spoon in the oatmeal.

"Xander's good, that's why—actually, he's the best I've worked with. There should be some perks to having a private detective in the family. But this has nothing to do with you or your choice in women. I get it. She's hot, and you're a living, breathing male, but you need to get real right quick on what happened the night you met her. You're in the public eye now more than ever and will have all kinds of women coming out of the woodwork, gunning for you and trying to get themselves attached to you."

He shoved a spoonful of oatmeal into his mouth as his dad stood there, and he wondered if he was waiting for him to say "Thanks, Dad." Instead, he felt sick, knowing what he did. At the same time, he wasn't too eager to pick up the phone and call Angie again. So what did that say?

"She was working the place," Neil said. "Seems she's got a dark side to her, because, as you read, she's a frequent flyer with the casinos, the bars, always leaving with a different guy. Seems you were just the pick of the night. Whatever her angle, you evidently were the one who bit. She just happened to get you drunk enough that she got you where she wanted you, at the altar and married." His dad filled a second mug with coffee and slid it in front of him. He scooped the last of the oatmeal and took a swallow of the coffee, noting the time. With the traffic, he needed to get going to the arena.

"You know what, Dad? I appreciate how you worry and think you need to protect all of us from everything and everyone as if they're going to take advantage of us, but you know, out of everything I read last night, I can't imagine the kind of life she had, growing up. It's just a report, and despite how neatly Xander reported all of it, it wasn't flattering. At the same time, she didn't have the kind of family I did. Reading everything she lived through without knowing any of what she actually had to experience, I'm sure I can understand only a tiny, tiny bit of how she felt. I honestly don't know, if that was my family, how I would've fared. I'm not saying it's an excuse, but out of all that crap, her life, her bad choices, even though it seemed she was heading nowhere, she got herself through school, got a degree, and became a teacher. Why?"

He swallowed the last of his coffee and set the mug down as he shook his head and took in his dad, the frown on his face, and that hard expression. He wasn't going to like what he was about to hear. "Why be a teacher?" Michael continued. "I guess I'd like to know why she chose that. I have my ideas, but they're mine, not hers."

"We're not even talking about that, and it's not the issue," Neil said. "You met her at a bar. The woman has some issues, evidently, and there is the fact you're now married to her. Xander talked to three of the bartenders, two of the wait staff, and the club owners and hotel staff who have seen her over several months. She worked you for that marriage proposal…"

He waved his hand to get his dad to stop. "And I was the drunk, working her to get her in bed. Yeah, I read all that, but I've got to go, so I'm done talking about this." He took in the mess on the counter, the dirty dishes he knew his dad was going to clean up, feeling more unsettled now than he ever had. "And, Dad, I know you want her gone and think that cutting her a check to pay her off is the answer for a quick annulment."

His dad stacked the bowl on the plate, then flicked his powerful, strong gaze over to him. "It is the answer, but the whole idea is to get a handle on how much it will take to get rid of her. She's in tough times. She's struggling, so I'm figuring ten thousand, no more than twenty. Start with ten, because she'll likely take that, knowing how desperate she is. She'll sign, and then you can be done with this."

He said nothing for a second as he took in the clock on the stove, knowing he had to leave, surprised by the lowball figure his dad had tossed out. That was chump change, a drop in the bucket for his dad, not the figure he'd have expected. "You know what? I'm going to think on that, on all of this. And, Dad, thanks again for breakfast and all this, but…"

Neil had an odd smile on his face as he took him in, shaking his head. "I know you want to get your own place, some dive."

"About Angie, Dad, I mean it. I'll handle it, sort it out," he said. This wasn't just a business deal, though he knew that was how his dad saw it. Neil wasn't emotionally involved, and it wasn't him who had woken up with a ring on his finger after a drunken night. This was all him, his problem, his to fix.

At the same time, he wanted the truth, the real truth of what he'd done, what she'd done. That wasn't something he was going to share with his dad, though.

Chapter Sixteen

____

Being on leave meant not earning an income, and that was on top of the shock of what had happened, the horror of being accused of the one thing she hadn't done.

Everyone in the school, the staff, the teachers, and likely all the parents would hear some version of Hasek's account of who she really was, and to make it worse, she expected her entire being would now be under a microscope for everyone to dissect. It was a good thing she had walked, though she couldn't remember the eight blocks back to the Airbnb. At least now she'd moved past the shock and betrayal to anger and could feel something other than wanting to cry her eyes out.

A man could just walk in and toss out a vile accusation, and no one had asked him for proof? In fact, they had taken his word alone because it was worth more than hers, because of his position, his money, and the fact that he knew people she didn't. What really made her angry was the fact that his moral character wasn't even in question. This friend who had supposedly picked her up as a hooker had urged Hasek to do the same, and she had no doubt he had in fact been out grazing for his own pick, yet that was okay? She squeezed her fists and cursed under her breath, going from hurt, to angry, to rock bottom, again having to fight the urge to cry.

What had her boss done but cave under the pressure to save her own skin? She'd worked with Erin over the past few years, and she'd been thrown under the bus because Hasek had threatened to go after her job. The biggest problem was that this all seemed to be just a repeat of her entire life.

She strode to the front door of the Airbnb and shoved the key in the lock, hearing the blast of the television.

"Hello," the deep voice called out as she stepped in, and the volume on the TV plummeted. Isaac Butterman, the owner of this less-than-stellar place, was reclined in his easy chair in the living room, the same spot he always sat, with a soda and a bag of nachos.

She didn't say anything as she strode in and took in the gameshow on the big screen. She wondered if he actually had a job.

"Wasn't expecting you till later. School out already?" he asked before shoving a handful of cheesy nachos into his mouth. He swiped the back of his hand over his dark moustache to wipe away the crumbs. His dark hair was wavy and in need of a wash, which had her cringing, as she was sharing the only bath with him. Yes, it had been far from clean.

"Done for the day," was all she said, forcing a smile to her lips, which ached because the urge to cry was starting to get the best of her. "So I know I only paid for three nights…" she started, then stopped as he lifted the soda and an iPad from the table beside him.

He tapped the screen as he took a swallow of the soda. "Got someone already booked for the weekend, then nothing next week. Are you looking at booking more nights?" he asked, peering at her over the iPad.

She knew he found her attractive, hot. It was in his eyes, his face, just something guys couldn't hide, and she knew he was waiting for her to answer. She should say no. "Well, if I can book a few more nights, just until I find something else…"

At least she would have time to look for something else and not grab the first thing because of the price. She was still having a hard time understanding how he could run an Airbnb and charge what he did, considering that what she thought was gray carpeting appeared as if it had never been vacuumed, the galley kitchen had two cupboard doors missing, and the fridge had been filled with containers of moldy food. Seriously, there had to be something better.

"Done, there. Charged your card. We're good to go. Listen, could cancel the weekend person if you want something more long term. I mean, I kind of like you, Angie, and I don't know these other people. Since I already have your deposit…" He flashed her a smile, and although she should have been creeped out, there was something about him that reminded her of her brother—useless, looking for an easy dollar, and letting life pass him by. It was sad, really.

"Just a few nights. Don't bother cancelling the others, as this is only temporary, as I said. Just trying to find a place to rent long term. This is just a temporary fix. Just to be clear, the deposit is refunded when I leave, right?"

"Yup, just to cover damages, but you seem pretty neat, so I can't see a problem. Will be sent to your card. Just allow five to ten business days, is all, before you see the credit."

She could feel her stomach tighten again, feeling the

loss of money that she needed more than ever. What was she left with? Not much. She squeezed her purse, feeling the vibration from her cell phone, so she reached in and pulled it out. She saw a text from Michael: *Call me. We need to talk.*

"Ah, you know what? I've got to make a call. Excuse me." She forced a smile to her lips and started to the bedroom.

"'Kay, just let me know if you change your mind. I'll bounce the weekend bookies and slot you in." Then he turned the volume back up on the gameshow as she stepped into her bedroom and closed the door, taking in the uncomfortable double bed with its ugly blue comforter and her two suitcases crammed in the small closet with no doors. She dialed Michael's number. Her heart was hammering as she listened to the ring.

"Hello?" he barked, and she had to cover her ear from the background noise on his end.

"Michael, it's Angie." She could feel her heart thumping in her throat and pressed her hand to her chest as she looked out the small bedroom window that faced a concrete wall.

"Hey, yeah, I called you a couple times and you didn't get back to me."

Actually, it was three times, but she'd been dealing with moving and the accusation, and she had refused to call him because of the urge to ask him to meet. She couldn't do that, knowing that next he would want the papers signed. Another ending to something that wasn't really real. Why did it feel as if everything was being taken from her? "Yeah, sorry, it's been a crazy few days."

"So did you find a place? Sorry about the way we left, and all."

There it was. What could she say? She looked around

at a room that was as basic as you could get. As she took in her suitcases, she realized the zipper of the big suitcase was facing the wall. She walked over to the closet, looking closer. "Yeah, an Airbnb until I can find something permanent… Son of a bitch!" She froze, feeling the horror of what she was seeing shoot right through her. The zipper wasn't fully closed, and her black dress, the backless one she'd worn only a handful of times, was stuck in it.

"What's wrong?" Michael asked on the other end as she lifted out her suitcase and pulled the zipper down carefully without wrecking her dress. Her clothes had been folded the wrong way, when she always rolled everything so it wouldn't be wrinkled. She glanced to the closed door and felt sick. That prick out there had gone through her things.

"Ah, just realized that the Airbnb owner went through my things, is all, like my day just couldn't get any worse." Could she not catch a break?

"Are you telling me someone went through your things?" Michael said. She didn't know him well, but she knew when someone was angry. She could hear it in the edge of his voice. "Is anything missing?"

She looked through her suitcase, seeing her underwear, her bras. Every part of her sensed he'd touched everything. She shivered as she unzipped her makeup bag, seeing the earrings, the necklaces of little value. Everything seemed to be there, but she held her breath as she rummaged the inside pocket of the suitcase and finally pulled out her mother's pearls. She sat on the bed, feeling weak and exhausted.

"I don't think so, but why would he go through my things, my underwear, my clothes? This is creepy," she said, for the first time noticing that the door didn't lock. There was no way she was spending another night in this place.

She'd rent a motel room if she had to. She'd already paid, though. Would she be able to get her money back?

"Who are you renting the place from? Do they live there, too? Like, what the fuck, Angie?" he stated, and she tucked the phone between her shoulder and head as she reached in the closet for her other suitcase and lifted it on the bed to unzip it.

"Some guy on the Airbnb site, a two-bedroom condo. He rents out one of the rooms. It's not much of a place. I'll get a motel tonight and find something else." She pressed her hand to the back of her head. "But I don't think that's why you called me, and I kind of knew this was coming. You want this marriage over, right?" She swallowed past the lump in her throat.

"This isn't a love match, Angie. It was one of those drunken things. Yes, a lawyer's done up the papers for an annulment, but I wanted to see if you need something, too. And this Airbnb guy, I could give him a call," he said.

She noted the hesitation, as she could feel the ending of something she hadn't even had a chance to get to know. She shook her head even though she knew he couldn't see her. "You don't owe me anything, Michael, and no, you don't need to call the guy. I'll just get my money back and leave. So how did you want to do this, mail, courier?" she said, opening her other suitcase. It seemed nothing had been touched.

"Your signature has to be witnessed, so let me make arrangements. I can't get away. I've got a game in Boston tonight and practice tomorrow, then some prior commitments I can't get out of. Unfortunately I don't have a free second, or I'd fly back there."

Of course, she should congratulate him on signing with the Canucks. He was officially in the limelight, but she didn't know how he'd take it, so she said nothing, even though the sports news reported everything. "It's fine," she said, feeling tears stinging her eyes and her throat starting to close up. "Look, I've got to get going."

"Hey, wait, at least let me pay for a hotel room for you until you can find something. I can do that much." He sounded so nice, and she wished this could be something, but these kind of good things didn't happen for Angie.

She should say no.

"Angie, come on, seriously. I still feel bad for how we left, and I wish I could be there and do something."

She could hear someone else talking in the background.

"Hey, listen, I've got to go. Let me book you a place. I'll send you a text of the hotel, and I'll call you after we land to see if you got checked in."

She stared at the closed door, feeling the creep on the other side, wondering if he could hear her talking. She didn't want to accept this even though she knew Michael was just relieved at being rid of her. A hotel would be nice for the night, a bath, a TV, and a moment to figure out what to do next.

"Okay, I'll talk to you later," she said and ended the call. Then she took in her open suitcases, feeling the betrayal, and yanked open the bedroom door. Isaac was laughing as he watched his gameshow on TV, and she stepped out of the room, feeling anger pumping through her veins, with every intention now of getting her money back.

Chapter Seventeen

He wondered how the married players did it. Between traveling to and from the arenas, airports, personal appearances, meeting with the media, working out, and the time they each needed to take to eat nutritious meals, there was very little left for much of anything else, yet many of the players had a wife and children, so they had to fit a home life in there somewhere.

That was one of the things Michael was struggling with as he rode with the other players to the airport, thumbing through his phone to book Angie a room at the Flamingo for four days. He texted her the reservation number. It was a nice place, a modest room, and he hoped she'd be comfortable while he figured out how to juggle the next few days, with practices, then charters to a new city, a game, trainers, media appearances, obligations to the team, and then the injuries that happened to all of them almost every game—bruises, pulled muscles. Part of the demands of being a pro hockey player was a tolerance for pain. They played hurt because injuries were part of the game, and if he couldn't play, someone else would.

Even though he was part of a team, he knew well that there was always that worry of how he would do on his next contract. Him being the newbie, he had a lot to prove, a lot to hold on to, which meant he needed to practice longer, harder than all of them, and never be first off the ice.

The plane touched down, and the players shuttled to the hotel, checked in, grabbed gear, and headed to the arena. After more ice time and practice, they were back at the hotel.

"Hey, Friessen, we're grabbing a drink before dinner! Join us," called Baker, the left wing, as Michael reached the elevator. Being part of the team meant he kind of needed to be part of the team.

"Got something to take care of first. I'll be down in a bit," he added, watching Baker along with six other guys from the team head into the bar. He jabbed the button and rode up with a few others to the tenth floor, which had been reserved for the entire team, and he was thumbing through his messages as he made his way to his room.

Nothing from Angie, and no answer to his text. After hearing about the Airbnb creep, he'd used the frustration he felt at wanting to wrap his hands around the guy's neck and had put it into his practice. He dialed her number as he dumped his gear at the door and listened to it ring, but it went right to voicemail.

"Hey, Angie, it's Michael. Just checking to see that you got my text and checked into the hotel. Give me a call back." He hung up, then pulled up the reservation confirmation and called the hotel.

"Hi, I made a reservation earlier today for my, uh…" He hesitated because she was his wife, yet he couldn't really refer to her that way. "My wife, Angie Debois. I just want to see if she's checked in yet." He rattled off the reservation number.

"Just a minute, sir. I'll check for you," the hotel clerk said.

He could hear a lot of background noise, hotel noise, life in Vegas, and he couldn't help wondering why Angie had picked Vegas to live. Having her sign that annulment would mean he wouldn't need to talk to her again, but he still had questions, and he wanted to know.

"No, I'm so sorry, sir, but she hasn't checked in yet. Can I take a message for her and give it to her when she does?"

Where the hell was she? She should have been there hours ago. "Yeah, just tell her to call Michael. She has my number." He tossed his phone on the bed and sat, then reached for it again and sent her a text. *Hey, where are you? You didn't check in. Starting to get worried.*

He waited, but there was no response. He didn't know where she'd been staying or where this Airbnb was, not that he could do anything from Boston. He pulled in a breath and then let it out, because if she hadn't checked in, how was he going to get her to sign annulment papers? Could she be looking for something more? He didn't think so, but he couldn't help feeling his dad's warning, and he considered his options.

He thumbed through the numbers on his phone and dialed, and it was answered on the second ring.

"Yup?" His deep voice was the same.

"Xander, it's Michael. I know my dad asked you to find out everything you could on Angie, the lady I…"

"Hey, yeah. I looked and dug. That's a crappy thing to wake up to, Michael," Xander said, cutting in. He wondered if he was waiting to rub in how stupid he was.

There was just something about Xander, but he and Michael had never clicked.

"Well, here's the thing. I'm not sure if my dad shared any of her plight with you, but she lost her place and was in an Airbnb. I booked a hotel for her, and she hasn't checked in. I'm worried because…" Because some guy was going through her things, or because all of this could turn into a scenario he wouldn't like?

"You think she skipped out or was looking to work an angle?" Xander said, getting right to it. He could hear the squeak of a chair in the background and knew he should ask about his sister, Cat, except Cat was a source of contention between them.

"I don't know. All I know is when I talked with her before I caught my flight to Boston, she'd just figured out the dirtbag who ran the Airbnb had gone through her things. She should have checked in, so if you could, like, do your investigative thing and find out where she is? Can you track her cell phone? I'll give you her number." He could hear the way Xander pulled in a breath and wondered if he'd tell him no.

"Officially, I can't track it," Xander drawled, "but give me the number, and I'll find her. You want me to tell you everything I find or sugar-coat it for you?"

"Fuck, Xander, just find her and tell me. I don't need you to sugar-coat anything," he snapped, knowing what Xander thought of him, which was not much.

"Great, consider it done. And, Michael, I'm just giving you a hard time, but word of advice? From what I read of the woman, and I've met many like her and have been doing this a long time, you need to end this quickly. Get her to sign, cut her a check, get her out of your life."

The last thing he wanted right now was a lecture from

Xander. "Thanks, Xander, but I have a father. Don't need to hear this again. Just let me know when you find her."

He knew he was being a prick, and he pressed end before Xander could tell him one more thing about how screwed up Angie was, or tell him how stupid he was. Listening to his dad tell him all the ways he'd fucked up was one thing, but listening to Xander was another.

Chapter Eighteen

There was something familiar about the clang of bars, the buzz of locks, and the sound of the county jail where she was stuck in a cell with eight other women. Three were prostitutes, one had embezzled money, one was a drunk passed out on a bench, one was in for narcotics, and the other two she couldn't remember.

She rubbed at the ink on her fingertips from where they'd fingerprinted her, all because of Isaac Butterman. She'd never get her job back now.

"Angie Debois," one of the guards called out as the cell door slid open.

She stood up, her hair a mess, because they'd taken her hair tie away along with her wedding ring and earrings. The guard was a large woman who had at least two inches on her and motioned for her to turn around. Cuffs were slapped on her again, twice in one day, but not the first time in her life.

"Your lawyer's here," the guard said.

She frowned. "I didn't call a lawyer because I can't afford one. You mean the public defender, don't you?"

That was impossible, though, because she'd meet them tomorrow at arraignment just a second before she saw the judge.

"Nope, an actual lawyer," the guard said as she led her to a concrete interrogation room with a steel door.

Angie took in the woman before her: light hair, older, a burgundy skirt and matching jacket, glasses.

"Thank you, officer," the woman said. "Can you take the cuffs off, please, so I can meet with my client?"

Was she in the wrong room? They must have mixed her up with someone else. She was about to say something when the cuffs came off, the guard left, and the door closed. She ran her hands over her wrists where the cuffs had been.

"Angie, come, have a seat. I'm Claire Duffin, with Seabreeve and Duffin. I was retained by your husband."

Angie took in the steel chair and was stuck on "husband." She wanted to point out her mistake. "I'm confused. What do you mean, my husband? I think there might be a mistake, here." She pulled out the chair and looked around at the steel mesh over the windows, another sight she'd hoped to never see again.

The lawyer had a file open and peered at her over the rim of her glasses. She pulled them off and sat back. "Michael Friessen, your husband?" she said. "I've been retained to get you out, at least on bail, and then sort this situation out, but first I'm going to need the details of what happened. Uttering threats, assault, and attempted theft? Not good, but I think I can make a case to at least get bail, and then we can work on getting the case dismissed. You're a school teacher with no priors…"

"I was in juvie as a kid," she interrupted and took in the surprise on the lawyer's face. She hesitated before she shook her head.

"Well, that's sealed and will have no relevance. So it says here in the officer's report that you threatened the owner of the Airbnb where you were staying. He said he feared for his life, and when the officers got there, the guy was on the floor, saying you shoved him."

Angie rolled her eyes, because that slimy prick had refused to refund her money for the additional nights, citing a seventy-two-hour cancellation window, which was bullshit. "He went through my things, my suitcases. I was leaving to stay in a hotel, and he refused to refund my money, so I picked up his iPad and threatened to smash it to bits. The only threat I uttered was that I wished all manner of horrible things to befall him and a speedy trip to hell. He grabbed my arm with his greasy hands, and I shoved him only to get away from him. Yeah, he fell, and I tossed his iPad on top of him as he carried on and yelled and called the cops, and I went to grab my things, but the cops arrived just as I opened the door to leave with my suitcases. The next thing, they arrested me, and here I am." She crossed her arms, feeling a chill in the room, and wished she had a sweater.

"Well, sounds simple enough, but unfortunately, the man insisted on being taken to the hospital and is complaining of a bruised tailbone. He's on bedrest. I think we'll at least be able to get you out tonight, though." She checked her watch. "The only issue could be your teaching until this is sorted out."

She bit down softly inside her cheek and then pulled in a breath. "You do know how Michael and I met? Our marriage isn't a real marriage, and today I pretty much lost my job and was accused of being a hooker by one of my students' fathers, who seems to have the kind of influence I don't, so there's no job to go back to right now. And this here…" She lifted her hand to take in the concrete cell.

"This seems to be just the way my day, my week, my life is going."

The lawyer put down her pen, shocked, and crossed her arms as she leaned back in her chair. "I think you'd better start at the beginning, Angie, and don't leave anything out."

Chapter Nineteen

She was in jail.

Michael was still trying to wrap his head around what Xander was saying as he gripped his soda water where he leaned against the bar. He was with his team, doing the social thing. He needed to be part of the team.

"You cool there, Michael?" Xander said. "Not sure if you heard what I said, but it looks like the cops were called in to break up an incident. Don't know all the details, but they're saying an unruly guest was caught stealing, became hostile, and assaulted the owner of the Airbnb."

He moved away from the bar and could hear a couple of the rowdy team guys call after him.

"Hey, Friessen! Come on, get back here and order a real drink," one of them called out and laughed.

He just shook his head and pulled the phone away as he tried to get his head around what Xander was saying. "Nope, done for the night! Got something to take care of," he added as he strode out of the bar, really digging into each step as he headed to the elevator, looking right and left to see who was around.

"Michael, you still there?" Xander said.

He pressed the phone to his ear as he jabbed the button to the elevator. "Yeah, here. I don't know what to say. It makes no sense. The dirtbag had gone through her things. That was why I booked her the hotel. She was leaving anyway to a motel, just… She did say she was going to ask for her money back. Shit!" The doors slid open, and he stepped into the empty elevator and closed the doors before anyone else could come in.

"Look, you asked me to find her, so I found her. Normally, under different circumstances, I'd say cut your losses. She made her bed, and you owe her nothing, but the problem is that legally, she's married to you, and since you're now in the public eye, you know, Michael Friessen, the hockey pro, even as twisted as it all is, I've got to point out to you the potential problem for you if the news picks this up, any of it. It could turn into a media shitstorm the likes of which you won't want. You just signed a contract, and this could cause problems for you."

Of course, he could hear the urgency. He was torn, because he wanted to help, but at the same time, he could hear his dad's warning, considering the report he'd already read of her past. He now really had more questions than answers. What he needed to do was sit down and talk to her, but it was an impossible situation, as he was here and she was there. The elevator stopped at his floor, and he stepped out.

"Well, what the hell am I supposed to do, get on a plane? I have a game tomorrow night. I can't just fly to Vegas to take care of this, because then I could lose everything," he snapped as he pulled his keycard out and tapped the door, furious. He didn't have time for this. He had a midnight curfew and early practice. Yeah, he was angry, and he realized he was angry at Angie…for what? For not just walking away, grabbing her bags, and getting out? He let the door close and sat on the edge of the bed.

"You get her a lawyer who handles this quietly," Xander said. "That's what you do. It gets her out of jail, and she can sit her ass in a hotel room until this goes away. I know you're not going to want to hear this, and it's much like a thorn in my ass to say it, but call your dad. Get Neil on a plane to Vegas to see to it that she doesn't get herself in any more trouble. Get her out of this mess. Then get that annulment signed, cut her a check, and make sure she's on her way. Then you cut ties, and whatever she does after that, it's got nothing to do with you."

He pulled in a breath. "Fine, I'll get a lawyer for her, and, Xander…" He didn't want to ask, but he needed to keep his focus here and didn't have a clue what else could come out of the woodwork.

"I'm waiting," Xander said impatiently in that arrogant way of his.

"Look, I know you think I'm some spoiled, privileged jock," Michael started, but he stopped when Xander laughed on the other end.

"You know what? Seriously, Michael, if that's what you think, then you don't really know me, but you really think this is the time for this?"

Fair enough. He stood up and paced the room. "Point taken. I guess I wanted to ask if you would consider maybe going to Vegas with my dad. You know, maybe there's something you could do to help. Actually, I'm sure you could do something." He wondered if Xander would say no. The fact of the matter was that he hadn't taken any time to get to know the guy his sister had fallen in love with and was living with.

There was a hesitation on the other end. "Of course I will. So you're going to call your dad, or do you want me to do it for you?" he added, and Michael wondered if this was his way of pointing out that he thought he was just a kid still.

"I'll call my dad. And, Xander..." He slid his fingers through his hair.

"Yeah?"

"Thank you."

"Well, it's the least I can do, since you're family."

Chapter Twenty

I t took her a minute to realize where she was when she woke up. The light streaming in reflected off the white walls as she lay in the most comfortable bed, much like the one that was in storage with all her things.

She was aware that Michael's father was on the other side of the doors, a man who had arrived when she'd stood before the judge and pled not guilty, then been released on a five-thousand-dollar bond, which apparently Neil had also paid. Here she was now, staying in a two-bedroom suite where he was bunking in the other bedroom with Xander, a dark-haired private detective who was, if she understood correctly, part of the family, involved with Michael's sister.

She slipped out of bed in her underwear and pulled on the hotel robe since she didn't have any of her suitcases still. Her long blond hair was a mess, and she wished for a brush or something but settled on running her fingers through it and tucking it behind her ears. She pulled open the door and stepped out, seeing both Neil and Xander up.

They were so different, but at the same time, they were both tall, dark, and handsome, dressed smartly, one more casual than the other, drinking coffee and eating what looked like room service.

Neil glanced up, but he didn't get up from where he sat on the sofa. "Great, you're up," he said. "There's coffee by the bar, and take your pick—fruit, muffins, toast." He gestured with his chin.

Angie wasn't sure what to make of the way Xander was watching her as he stood up, went to the bar, and poured coffee in a mug, then handed it to her, black.

"Thank you," she said as she put the mug down and reached for the cream. She could feel him watching her. She didn't bother to stir it.

"Claire is on her way over," Neil said, "and Michael called earlier for you. He wants to talk to you."

He'd called last night, too, after they'd checked in, but she'd refused to speak with him. She wasn't sure what to make of the way his father watched her. This was humiliating, but she'd be damned if she'd show it.

"I appreciate all this, and the lawyer," she said. "I'm unclear as to why you're doing all this, though," she said before she lifted the mug, swallowed, and took in both Xander and Neil and the way they watched her. She was still unsettled after everything she'd shared with Claire, her lawyer.

"You're married to Michael, and this situation is something that could affect him," Neil said, and she got it in that second. This was about protecting his image. Good thing they didn't know what had happened with the school. She had to look away as she felt the emotion of all of this burn her eyes. She blinked as she made a point of turning her back and walking over to the desk, pulling the chair out, and sitting down.

"Then there's the matter of your school," Neil added, and she noted something that passed between him and Xander. Boy, they had to believe she was an absolute fuck-up. If it was her in their shoes, she'd likely think the same thing.

"I see," was all she could get out, all she wanted to say. "Did Claire tell you?" She needed to know. Maybe confidentiality applied only to the person paying the lawyer's fees, but at the same time, she knew that wasn't true.

"Claire hasn't shared anything," Xander said. "That was all me. Found out you were let go yesterday. Your leave of absence is about to be permanent because you were accused by a parent of escorting at hotels."

She wondered by the way he watched her whether he believed it. Of course they both did. "Does Michael know?" she asked. They had to hate her for who she was. She swallowed past the lump that was now wedged in her throat.

"Yup, told him this morning," Neil said. "He's calling again after practice. He's got a game tonight. So did you do it?"

Xander was watching her too. She shouldn't care what they thought.

"No, I'm not a hooker," she stated, "if that's what you're asking. Or are you asking whether I assaulted a man who has a hundred and fifty pounds on me, who rummaged through my things, my underwear? Did he take something? I don't know, because I don't have my suitcases, my things. He does. Did I threaten to hurt him? I don't know. I guess that's up to interpretation. I did wish him a speedy trip to hell." She didn't miss the way Xander's mouth crooked as if fighting a smile.

"You could have just left," Neil said, sitting, watching her, and she knew he wished his son had never met her.

"Really? I was staying in an Airbnb because I can't find a place I can afford to rent—not just the rent but all the deposits they want. I paid upfront for additional nights. I wanted my money back after he invaded my privacy. I needed that money, he refused, and…"

"You, what, threatened him?" Neil cut her off. Xander turned to him from where he leaned against the sofa table. She wondered what that was about.

"No, I grabbed his iPad, the one that had all my credit card info, the one he used for bookings. I was angry because the jerk would have used it to charge me more. I don't know, but before I could finish getting out, I wanted him to remove my information. He grabbed my arm." She lifted her left arm, where she could see the imprint of fingers. The bruising was subtle but there. "I fought him to get his hands off me, and yeah, I shoved hard, and he fell backwards, knocking stuff over and carrying on and on. He called the cops, and by the time I was opening the front door to leave, the cops were there. Now here we are," she said.

There was a knock at the door of the suite. Xander answered it, and again she didn't know what to make of the way Neil was watching her, so she pulled her gaze away and lifted her coffee, taking another swallow, feeling the pangs of hunger. She stood up, walked over to the bar, and took a muffin.

"Here're your suitcases," Xander said as he carried them into the room. "Have a look through them and see if there's anything missing. Claire talked to the cops and arranged to get your things back."

There was another knock at the door, and this time Neil got up and answered it. Claire was there, and Angie watched as she shook hands with Neil and then stepped into the suite.

"Good morning, Angie. Hey, I have great news for you," she said after declining a coffee from Neil and resting her briefcase on the sofa table.

Angie said nothing as she waited, holding that muffin. She gave in and took a bite—blueberry bran, she thought. Yum. She could feel Xander behind her and glanced back to see him standing just outside her room.

"Charges were dropped," Claire said. "It seems Mr. Butterworth agreed to drop them all, citing a difference of opinion, if you won't seek money from him or a refund. You'll basically go your separate ways."

Was she serious? "So what you're saying is that I'm supposed to just let him keep the money I paid after he went through my things, money for nights I didn't stay in his dump? Then there's the deposit I paid. Does he get to keep that, too?" She could feel the way her heartbeat kicked up, knowing that if she were smart, she'd take the win, but it wasn't a win to her.

"It's a small price to pay, Angie, and this all goes away," Neil added, turning to the lawyer. "Take it. Make this happen."

"No," she said, then took in the surprise on everyone's faces.

"What do you mean, no?" Claire said.

"I mean no, I won't let him take one dime. I'm tired of being taken advantage of by unscrupulous scumbags, so no, he doesn't get to keep my money. That's my money that I earned and I worked damn hard for. To you all, it may seem like nothing, but it's everything to me."

She wasn't sure who was more surprised, but she'd be damned if she let that prick walk away with what was hers. This was his win, not hers.

"It's like a few hundred, Angie," Neil said. "Just let him have it."

"Actually, it's $586.23, with tax, which included my deposit, and I want it back." She wasn't going to give in.

"I'll give you the money, then," Neil snapped, and she could see he was pissed off.

"No," she said again. He appeared ready to argue, so she lifted her hand. "If I have to go to jail for something I didn't do, fine, but no way in hell is he getting away with not paying me back. He owes me, not you. If you don't mind, I'm going to check my suitcases and see if there's anything missing, then take a shower." She lifted the muffin and shoved it in her mouth, taking another bite as she took in the shock on everyone's faces.

"Angie, that's ridiculous," Claire said as if she wanted to pull her aside and shake her. "You would go to jail for a few hundred dollars? You'd have a record, and you'd never be able to teach. Jail is no picnic…"

"Look, Angie, I get it," Xander interrupted and took a step closer to her. "You're pissed and have every right to be. The guy's a scumbag jerk, but take my advice: Walk away, chalk it up to a bad lesson learned. I hear your anger, and I'm with you. I agree, and I get it, but the way this went down, sometimes it's best to take a step back and take the win even though it doesn't seem like it."

She knew Xander was trying to convince her, and she knew the only reason was to get the charges dropped so none of this could stain Michael.

The phone was ringing again, and Neil answered. She wasn't sure who he was talking to, but he walked her way and held it out.

"It's Michael," he said. "He wants to talk to you."

She put down her coffee, took the phone, and walked into her bedroom, where she closed the door. She took a minute as she sat on the bed and pressed the phone to her ear. "Hi, Michael," she said, hearing background noise—the arena, she thought.

"Are you okay? You didn't call me back," he said, and she didn't miss the concern.

"Yeah, I am now. I guess I have you to thank for the lawyer, your dad, and Xander. I'm sorry, I just didn't want to talk to you. It was kind of a crappy day." She knew he was waiting for something else.

"So what happened at school? Dad said that you were fired and accused of being…"

She just shook her head. "I was accused of being a hooker, Michael, but seems that no one needs any proof anymore." She stared at the muffin, and he said nothing. "If you want to know if it's true, no. I'm not a hooker."

There was silence for a minute. "You know what?" he said. "I have to get going, but I guess I kind of wanted to know one thing. Would you tell me the truth if I ask?"

She shut her eyes and wondered what it would be. "Yes. What is it you want to know?"

"Why were you at the hotels, the bars? Why were you seen with so many men, leaving with men?"

"The real reason?" She allowed the phone to slip down, then said, "Because I couldn't afford to eat. I would dress the way a guy wants to see me, the way you wanted to see me, your hands all over me. They would buy me a drink, dinner, and yes, they always expected more, but they didn't get it."

Except for Michael.

"Okay, listen, I've got to go, but we still have some things to settle," he said.

She nodded because she knew what he wanted. "I know, the annulment. Just send the papers. I'll sign what you need."

"Angie," he said again in the phone, and there was something about his deep voice that was making her more sad than anything.

"Yes, Michael?"

"I'm glad you're okay."

Chapter Twenty-One

They'd won their away game with a final score of six to five, and rookie player Michael Friessen had five shots on goal and had brought it all home with the final winning shot seconds before the buzzer went. His adrenaline surged with that raw excitement that filled every pore when he won big. This was just one of those moments he knew he would remember forever.

It had been his first game, his first big win in the big leagues, and he hadn't been just a player who floated by. He'd been one of the players who shined. He'd kept his head in the game and his problems off the ice.

That was why he found himself in a post-game interview outside the locker room with a microphone in his face, sweaty, needing a shower, and damn proud of himself. He wondered if his family was watching at home. Of course they were.

"How does it feel to be the newest member of the team and to bring in the winning goal seconds before the clock runs out?" the slick reporter asked. He was polished, flashy, and Michael couldn't remember what station he was from. The lights and camera were on him.

"It feels fantastic, but it comes down to the Canucks giving me the chance and signing me to the team. They believed I have what it takes to be a strong team player." Great answer. He wanted to pat himself on the back, thankful now that his dad had made him take the time to learn how to speak to the media so he wouldn't appear like an idiot. Players got only one shot, and if he blew it, the reel would play over and over again.

"So what makes you a strong team player? I mean, how do you just show up on the team and outshine some of the older senior players?"

"Well, I think you're misreading it a bit. I'm not outshining. I'm part of a team, and just like the rest of my team, to get where we are, we have to be the best and not be scared to take that shot. We all had the same discipline, starting out like every other kid playing the house leagues, traveling, getting up at five a.m. on the weekends to get to the cold rink, and we practice every day, improving our game. It just happened tonight I got the puck, the shot opened for me, and I didn't hesitate. I took it."

The man was nodding, and he wanted to say thank you and end this so he could shower and change and get to the airport for their midnight charter home. "Thank you, but I've got to get showered," he said. He was about to take a step away.

"Just one more question. Can you comment on the reports we received about your wife in Vegas who was arrested yesterday for assault, theft, and uttering threats? You were married just under a week ago. Were you aware of her history and the fact that she was fired from her job as a teacher because of rumors that she was working as an escort?" The microphone was in his face again, and he could feel all eyes on him.

"That's it for questions! We have a flight home to catch." His coach, Ron Hundleston, balding, older, and with a bad-ass attitude, shoved him aside and had all the cameras on him now. Michael slipped into the locker room, knowing that everyone on the team who didn't know already would soon.

"Friessen!" Hundleston called out.

Michael yanked off his jersey and glanced up as the coach made his way over. Two of the other players were heading to the shower, butt naked, as he sat on the bench and unlaced his skates.

"Great game tonight, but that little media frenzy out there about your wife? You need to take care of it."

He knew by his tone it wasn't just a suggestion.

"It's being handled now," he said, and Hundleston nodded.

"Let's be clear about optics. The higher-ups have a vision for this team, and it doesn't look favorable for a team member to have a problematic home life. Fans don't like those kind of optics, and those kinds of accusations about your wife won't go over well, so you need to fix them. Don't care how, but fix them. This is going to be a media circus, and right now our media people are going to need to fix this and put a spin on it. Get changed, because you aren't on the plane with the rest of the team. You're on your way back to Vegas to sort out this mess. A rep will be with you to advise you on a course of action and sort out a favorable outcome."

He didn't bother trying to explain, because Hundleston wasn't a man who wanted an explanation. He'd made clear what he wanted to happen. Why was it that nobody seemed to care what was true and what wasn't? He dumped his skates on the ground when the coach rested his hand on his shoulder.

"Hey, we've all had something. Just saying you need to fix this. Quite a way to start out a new marriage," he said before he walked away, and Michael wondered what he'd say if he knew what had really happened.

SHE COULD HEAR voices from the living room of the suite. Maybe that was what woke her. She looked at the clock beside her, which flashed after midnight. There was a knock on her door, and she pressed the sheet to her chest even though she was wearing a sleeveless nightgown. She sat up and flicked on the bedside lamp. "Just a minute," she said as she put her feet on the light carpeting.

"It's Michael."

She heard his voice and climbed from bed, reaching for the housecoat before pulling open the door, and she just stood there, looking up at tall, dark, and handsome, dressed in a dark suit, his white dress shirt collar open. Damn, he looked good, and she had to remind herself that even though she was married to him, she wasn't, not really. She could see his dad in the other room, the living room, but he stepped into the other bedroom and shut the door.

"Hi, uh, what are you doing here?" she said. She didn't know what to do and ran her hand over her hair, knowing it was a mess. She'd washed it, dried it, and hadn't bothered doing anything else to it.

"We need to talk." He gestured into the bedroom, and she glanced behind her to the king bed she'd just been sleeping in.

She stepped back, and Michael followed her in and closed the door. She said nothing because she didn't have a clue what to say, what he wanted. He wasn't supposed to be there.

"I'm going to get right to it," he said. "The media picked up on your arrest, caught me off guard after the game, but they're also reporting about the allegations and that you were fired from school."

She knew her mouth gaped as she pressed her hand to the flat of her chest. It wasn't supposed to be like this. Now her very private humiliation was public for everyone to scrutinize. She could feel the door closing permanently on any chance to move anywhere and start over.

"I'm sorry," he said.

"Why are you sorry?" She didn't mean for it to come out so sharply. "It wasn't you who supposedly did all this, not that it matters now."

He took a step toward her and rested his hands on her shoulders. "Angie, I spoke with the lawyer, and my dad said that you refused to take the offer. There would be no charges. It would all go away," he said.

She could feel the heat from his touch, the way it was affecting her. She wanted to shut her eyes and lean into that strength, because for a time she wanted to believe he cared. She took a step back, and his hands fell away.

"And he keeps my money? No, it's not right. He's the one who broke the supposed law, but in the eyes of the law, it was twisted around to me. How does something like that happen? No, I won't let him have the satisfaction. He's a sleazebag who just wanted the money, and if you say to me too that you'll give me the money…" She pressed her lips together hard and lifted her hand as she took a step back, shaking her head. There was no way in hell she was going to budge, not on this. It seemed to be her lot in life: Men seemed to always see her as a plaything, to find a way to work her into bed, or to take something from her. She was done with that.

His expression softened, and she didn't know what to make of it. "I get it, and I'm with you. I agree that he should pay, and it should be him sitting with his ass in jail on charges. I know when I called you how upset you sounded, and I was worried when you said he'd gone through your things. I wanted you out of there, and if I'd been here…" He gestured, and she could see how his expression changed, almost angry.

"If you'd been there…what, Michael? I don't understand how this is your problem. It's not on you, none of this," she added.

His hazel eyes seemed to flicker with fire, with a spark. Strength oozed through him. She hardly knew him, but at the same time, after everything that had happened, he wasn't behaving how she expected.

"But it is on me, Angie. I wasn't here to get you out of there, and then there's your school. When I called you yesterday when you were at the Airbnb, what went down at the school had already happened?"

Of course it had. She nodded and had to swallow past the lump in her throat.

He nodded. "Why didn't you tell me when I phoned? Why didn't you tell me what happened? You said nothing about losing your job and what this man accused you of."

The way he was staring at her so intently, she wondered if deep down he considered the possibility that it might be true.

"I was shocked, stunned, horrified," she said. "It's been many years since I was looked down on as if I was nothing, and maybe I didn't want you to know. There would've been no reason for you to know. After all, I'm signing your annulment, or have you forgotten we're going our separate ways?"

He still hadn't said anything, and then he looked around the room before settling his powerful gaze on her again. He took a step closer and another to close the gap between them. "Well, about that… See, here's the thing. Because of the media frenzy, an annulment now wouldn't work."

She just stared at him, and it took her a second to realize this was about him, not her. "So let me get this straight. This is about me, a nobody, but because we're married, it's now a problem for you."

He pulled in a breath but didn't step back, and an odd smile touched his lips as he shook his head. "Here it is, baby: We're married. You got screwed, and you need to take the deal, and the school thing? You need me to make it go away. It sucks big time, and if I were you, I'd be pissed too. This is the honest truth. I know you want justice, but I've got to tell you, sometimes life sucks, and the win in this is to take the deal to make this go away. Stop looking at it like he's getting away with screwing you, because I promise you he's not. One thing my dad has taught me is that when you're backed into a corner, you need to be smarter than your opponent. That douchebag will get his. We'll find a way to nail his ass after everything is fixed, after all this goes away, and no one is trying to imply that you're something you're not or you've done something you didn't."

This time, he did step back, and he slipped off what she knew was an expensive tailored suit jacket, tossed it on the chair, and ran his fingers through his hair.

"I don't understand what you're saying or what this is," Angie said. She didn't move as he again stepped closer to her and rested his hands on her shoulders, over her arms.

"We're married. Circumstances have changed. We

need to stay married, and that means appearances, media… and when we get this all sorted out, I want you to move to Vancouver with me."

This couldn't be real. She started to shake her head.

"Michael, as much as I want this, you're right about one thing: It was a mistake. You don't even remember getting married, saying I do. It was a drunken idea. I knew how drunk you were. I knew who you were, a hockey player who wanted me. Yes, you wanted me in your bed, so I dropped the one line I knew would have you walking away. I said I would only get into bed with a ring on my finger, because I wasn't that kind of girl. But you didn't leave. You said, 'Let's do it,' and you had us in that cab and bought that package…" She stopped because she expected outrage, shock, anger. This had been on her. Even though she'd had a lot to drink, she hadn't been drunk to the point that she didn't know the consequences of her actions. But he wasn't looking at her like that.

Instead, his hands rubbed her shoulders, and he took her in, her expression, all of her. "Kind of figured that, but it's not all on you," he said. "You didn't dump the liquor down my throat. I have some responsibility, but all of that is kind of moot anyway. We're married. Look, let's just fix this with you, move up to Vancouver, and everything else…we'll figure it out." He slid his hands over her shoulders and up to her face and just held her. "Say yes, Angie."

She pulled in a breath, really wanting to. "But we don't know each other, and you want to play house?"

He shrugged. "Well, I'd say that at least out of all this, we'll get to know each other. We're two strangers who got married, so what do you say if we start dating?"

He was crazy. For a minute, she wanted to ask if he'd been drinking again.

"Come on, Angie," he said. "I'm waiting."

"You promise me that Isaac won't get away with what he did?"

Michael shook his head. "I swear."

She considered for a minute. "Well, I guess I'm moving to Vancouver," she said, and he smiled that handsome, irresistible smile, and then he leaned in and kissed her. It was so gentle, so real, and he was sober.

Chapter Twenty-Two

The cameras flashed as he signed a dozen pucks for the kids in Angie's kindergarten class. Actually, it was their parents who wanted the signed pucks, not the kids, but it was all about optics.

"Michael, so how did you and Angie meet?" asked the man standing beside the principal, Erin Brown. Even though she seemed nice, pleasant, it wasn't lost on him how she'd thrown Angie under the bus.

"I was in town for a celebration and saw her across the room, and she took my breath away. The rest is history," he stated as he glanced over to Angie, who was dressed in beige capris and a white sleeveless blouse, appearing very much a kindergarten teacher. She was over at the side of the room with Xander and his dad. She was gorgeous, and she was playing a role for him.

"Is it true that Miss Debois is leaving?" one of the little kids asked, a girl with glasses, dark hair, and her two front teeth missing.

"Yes, I'm sorry," Michael said. "I know you all love having her as your teacher, but she's my wife, and we live in Vancouver now. I need her with me. It's selfish, but she'll get a job there teaching kindergarten to lots of lucky kids just like you."

He listened to the laughter from the parents as a few of the kids booed.

"Okay, that's it for questions," his publicist stated. "We have time for photos, and then Mr. and Mrs. Friessen have to catch a flight to Vancouver…"

The cameras flashed as she arranged him and Angie with the principal.

"I'm just so thrilled to meet you in person, Michael," Erin said, "and I am so glad everything has worked out. Angie, it really did upset me to no end. I lost sleep over those accusations Mr. Hasek made about you. I'm just so glad it's all worked out—and that you really are married to Michael Friessen."

Angie only nodded, and damn, he was proud of her. In the past few days, Xander had dug up a big neon skeleton from Mr. Thomas Hasek's closet. The city's architect was married to a dentist and had two kids, but he had a predilection for street walkers, preferably tall, leggy blondes who were trans.

"We're going to miss you, Angie," Erin said. "I wish you all the best." She actually hugged her, a hug Angie didn't return, and then walked away.

Michael reached for her hand, taking in the big diamond he'd bought her. "You handled that well," he said in a low voice and didn't miss the way she rolled her eyes.

"I did my part," she said, then leaned in. "So…how do you suppose that photo of Thomas Hasek with that hooker ended up on the news?" She flicked her gaze up to his and then over to where his dad and Xander were standing.

"Does it matter? I don't know about you, but seeing

him have to publicly resign from office seems like justice to me," he said.

She nodded. "And Isaac Butterworth?"

"It'll happen. One thing at a time, but first, are you ready to go home?" he asked, and she slid her other hand in his as the camera flashed.

"Yeah," she replied. "Vancouver, here we come."

Chapter Twenty-Three

He was good.

Michael knew exactly what to say to the press as Angie stood in the background during the morning media conference in Vancouver, fielding questions about her arrest and insinuations that he had married a hooker. He again denied it all.

"He's a natural, you know," said Nina Malone, the team's head of media, whom Angie was positive was behind this "staying married" thing, which Michael insisted had to happen.

"So do you think the media will ever let this go?" Angie asked.

Nina just tossed her an odd look, the smile she offered everyone as if it were part of her job. "It always dies down. He's addressed it and likely will again. It's only been a few days, but tomorrow there will be something else. You being here with him shows that what he's saying is true, and the stuff in Vegas is just rumors. Some will believe there's something to it, but at the same time, with everything going on in the world, you'll soon be forgotten. In this case, that's a good thing."

Nina patted her arm, and she realized Michael was done and was walking her way. She wondered whether she'd ever get used to how good he looked. With the body of an athlete and a tailored suit, her husband turned not only every other woman's head but hers, as well, even though none of this was real.

"You ready to get out of here?" Michael said, reaching for her hand. She nodded, knowing everyone was watching, as he leaned in and kissed her, quick, hurried, but still filled with heat. How did he do it? She wasn't as great at pretending.

He walked her out, her heels clicking on the floor. She was dressed in a beige tunic that stopped at her knees and a white sleeveless knit cardigan. Even this had been orchestrated: feminine, conservative, and not slutty.

She got it. Michael was living the life of an NHL player, and the fact was that he didn't have a day off—from games, to daily practices, to meetings with his trainer, to media appearances. Then there were team meetings with the coach, more media, and more practice, not to mention the food and how healthy he ate. How many more months of this were there until the season ended? It would be like this for a solid eight months of the year, and she didn't think anyone could understand the demands. She did now.

"So we're always under the spotlight?" she said, slipping on a pair of sunglasses as they walked across the parking lot to his SUV.

"Kind of goes with the territory," Michael said as he opened the passenger door for her, and she slipped inside. He closed it and waved to a few of the other players. She'd met them before, said hi and shaken their hands, but she wondered, from the looks they gave her, whether they believed she was in fact an escort. Maybe she was just being paranoid.

Michael slid behind the wheel and backed out, and she sighed.

"You okay?" he asked.

She flicked her gaze to him, taking in the sunglasses that covered his eyes, and wondered what he was thinking. "Yeah, just glad that's over. So am I expected to keep showing up for these media events?"

He maneuvered them onto the freeway, into the thick of traffic. He wasn't smiling, and she was having a hard time getting a read on him. "For now, yes, as long as the publicist says so. So how's the job hunt going?"

What could she say? It wasn't. "Unfortunately, teaching here in BC isn't going to happen. Just heard this morning that I'd have to complete a new teacher education program, because my certificate from Nevada isn't recognized here. I guess I may have to look at other options— like bartender, waitress, or stripper," she added, then wasn't sure what to make of the expression on his face. "Sorry, bad joke."

This time, the hint of a smile touched his lips. "Well, then, what about taking some classes or something?"

She knew he was just trying to help. He took the turnoff to the condo, the one his dad had bought and which they were living in. It was nice, and she was still getting used to the fact that she didn't have to worry about paying rent or keeping a roof over her head. She wondered if he'd ever be able to understand. Maybe not.

"I like being a teacher, Michael, but getting the certi-fication here could be a really long process." *And costly,* she thought. Maybe he didn't realize education wasn't free.

"How about tutoring or something in the meantime? I

mean, I'm going to be gone a lot, so you'll have a lot of time on your hands."

She wasn't sure what to say as he turned into the lot and pressed the button on his visor to open the garage door.

"Are you worried I'll get into trouble, embarrass you or something?" she said as he drove in and parked.

He turned his gaze to her, pulled off his sunglasses, and tucked them onto the visor. "I never said that and wasn't thinking it. This is about you having something to do. Maybe in the meantime, a charity would be a good idea. I'll call Nina and get her to hook you up with something. Charity is always a great PR thing."

He stepped out of the SUV and then opened the back and pulled out his gear. He was already inside by the time she stepped out of the SUV, and while she stepped out of her heels, he dumped his training jersey into the washer and started it. As she closed the door, she listened to the TV flick on to the news.

"Steak for dinner, Angie," he called out, and she could hear him in the kitchen, where he dumped the butcher-wrapped steaks on the counter. As he unbuttoned his shirt and climbed up the stairs, she knew she couldn't pretend anymore, and she followed him up. He walked into his bedroom to change, and she walked into hers.

Chapter Twenty-Four

Angie was holding on to something, and tonight Michael was determined to break down her walls or at least make a crack in them so she would open up a bit more. She was complicated, not the woman he'd thought she was. In a matter of days, they had gone from getting an annulment to living in Vancouver together, but she wasn't in his bed.

She strode into the kitchen in a pair of gray lounging pants and a hoodie, her hair damp from the shower. He was searing the steaks, the salad was already made, and the baked potatoes he'd opted for instead of a side of pasta were keeping warm in the oven.

"Smells good," she said as she slid onto a bar stool at the counter. "Hope one of those steaks isn't for me. There's no way I can eat all that."

"Eat what you can," he said. "I'll put the rest in the fridge as a snack for later."

He pulled the steaks from the pan and rested them on a plate as she took in the food, the broccoli and carrots he'd cut, ready to sauté in some butter and olive oil. Thanks to his dad, his fridge was well stocked.

She said nothing, and he wasn't sure what to make of her. He took in the baggy outfit, knowing how thin she was, reminding himself now that there was a difference between a slim, sexy woman and one who was a little too thin. Knowing more about her situation had him seeing her differently.

"So you mentioned me doing some charity work," she said. "I'm not earning an income, Michael, and the way things are shaking out, there may be a lot of hoops to jump through. The courses cost money, you know, and although I have some left…"

She stopped talking, and he got it. He didn't know why he hadn't figured it out before. Of course, she had next to nothing.

"I'll pay for it. Not a big deal," he said. "Besides, it might be good. I know a few of the wives are involved with kids' charities, and being a kindergarten teacher would make you a great fit. There's the Humane Society, too." He dumped the veggies in the heated pan and took in Angie as she walked barefoot to the cupboard and pulled out plates, knives, and forks.

"You want to pay for my school now?" she said.

He wasn't sure what to make of her tone as he plated up their steaks and sautéed veggies. "Of course, but if you want to wait and do the charity thing, that may work too. Maybe you want to think about it," he said as he slid both plates on the island.

She grabbed the salad dressing from the fridge and tossed him a glance, her face free of makeup. He took in how blue and bold her eyes were. Her lips were soft and pink, and it wasn't lost on him that he tasted them only when he kissed her for everyone to see. Behind closed doors, they had a completely different relationship.

"You think a kids' charity is a great idea with my past and with all the allegations about me? Even though you're working the media to convince everyone otherwise, I can't help thinking that maybe some of your teammates believe the worst of me. Nice job, though. Even I was starting to believe you. Maybe the Humane Society would be a better fit for now."

He'd just pulled the hot potatoes from the oven and put them on their plates, and he had to shake the burn from his hands, stuck on what she'd said. Was there something she wasn't telling him? "What are you talking about? Of course the guys on the team don't believe any of that. Did something happen, someone say something?"

She just shook her head as she sat at one of the bar stools and lifted her gaze. "I'm just very aware of how men look at me and see me."

What the hell did that mean?

He sat beside her at the island and wasn't sure what to make of her comment, so he just jabbed his knife in the baked potato and sliced it open, then took a hunk of butter from the container Angie slid in front of him. "I think you may be reading too much into it," he said. "You're attractive."

Maybe he needed to see to it that his team understood she was his wife, and him being part of the team meant they needed to have her back, too. She said nothing and took a small bite of her steak.

"I'm also curious why you think it would be best to steer clear of kids' charities," he said. "You like kids, being a teacher, so I think you would have a lot to offer. Angie, I think you're not giving yourself enough credit. I mean, look at what you've accomplished, considering your background and what you came from, what you overcame."

She stilled as she forked up her salad, and he realized his mistake, what he'd said. Before she could take a bite, she slid around on the bar stool. "What do you mean, what I overcame?"

When was a good time to bring up the background info Xander had dug up on her, the report he'd read? He'd somehow expected her to be okay with it. When his father had it done, it had seemed appropriate because they were going to be walking away from each other, but now he couldn't shake what a betrayal it seemed to be.

"Michael, what are you saying?" she urged him.

He shoved a piece of steak in his mouth and chewed as he tried to come up with something reasonable, to figure out how to tell her he knew all the details of a past she likely never wanted anyone to know. He put his fork down. "I guess this would be a good time to tell you that before this, before you living here, when we were getting this annulled, Xander did a background check on you."

He wasn't sure what to make of her face, how she stilled.

"You investigated me?"

He pulled in a breath. "Don't be mad, Angie. You'd have done the same in my shoes."

She scooted back her stool and stepped down. "No, I wouldn't have." She leaned in, her hands on the island, and then made a rude noise. "Why would you do that?"

What could he say? His dad had needed to make sure they knew what they were up against, as he'd seen her as the enemy, but there was no way he could say that. What had been the case then wasn't now.

"Because I didn't know you, and we ended up married," he said. "You were a stranger, but let's put that aside for now. I know you had a crappy childhood, spent time in juvie, yet you found a way to pull your life together, go to college, be a teacher. Why did you pick teaching?"

She crossed her arms, and he could see she was still mad, but at the same time, she was thinking, hopefully enough that she'd get past what he'd done. He couldn't deny he was glad his father had asked Xander to investigate her. For a minute, he wondered whether she'd answer.

"I don't know," she said. "Mainly I thought about helping kids, wanting to make a difference since I'd had to figure everything out myself. It wasn't so much about molding young minds but teaching them that they can have what they want and to dream big, to not let barriers hold them back. I didn't have that. My teachers never noticed, never saw I was hurting and in trouble. I'm sure you also saw how ill equipped my parents were for parenthood. I wanted to be the one adult a kid could come to, talk to. I found my way out, and I wanted to be that beacon for other kids. Not all would need it, but there's always that one. Is that lame? I really love teaching kids. It was just an a-ha moment. I knew I would be good at it."

He took her in and was having a hard time reconciling the outfit he had met her in with the image of her as a schoolteacher. "It's not lame," he said. "It just doesn't fit with the image of the woman at the bar. They're opposites. You spent time in juvie, you and your sister? Yeah, I read about your brother and sister, your parents, your life. Sorry about your mom."

She just stared at him and then pulled in a breath. "But you investigated me," she said. "I'm not sure how to feel about it."

He put his fork and knife down. "I'd do it again, Angie. I don't mean that to sound hurtful, but if I hadn't read that report and seen everything, all the accusations would've had me wondering, too."

Her face paled. She was taking it the wrong way, or maybe the right. "I see," she said. "Then I guess that makes it perfectly all right. Anything else you want to know?" She allowed her hands to fall to her sides, and he could see the way she balled them up. She was working her way toward being furious. Could he blame her? Then she lifted her hands in the air and backed up, turned, and left.

Her plate was still full. He sliced a piece of steak and shoved it in his mouth, hearing her on the stairs, then put down his fork and knife and stood up. What was he doing? He took in the silence, feeling the anxiety, the emotion ramping up in his condo, and he suddenly felt his back was against the wall. He'd had enough of tiptoeing around. Here they were, married, playing a role, fighting about something he'd never considered talking about. He went to the stairs and looked up just as she strode into her room, the one that wasn't his, and closed the door.

He considered what to do: leave her be or get in her face and have it out, settle all of this? If he was smart, he'd walk away—but apparently he wasn't that smart, because he was taking the stairs two at a time, feeling his adrenaline race, fire flickering inside him.

He put his hands on the knob of her closed door, considered what he was doing for only a second, and then turned the knob only to find that it was locked.

Well, shit! Now what?

Chapter Twenty-Five

"Angie, open the door."

She couldn't believe he was outside her bedroom door, pounding on it again. She took in the knob as he tried to turn it, but of course he couldn't get in, as she'd locked the door. She leaned against the dresser, the light wood, and took in the queen bed with its peach duvet. The room was done in warm tones and was comfortable, but at the same time, it was plain, because it had none of her personal things—her photos, her books.

"Angie, this isn't the way to handle things. I get that you're mad over what I did, but ask yourself what you would've done in my shoes. You don't know me, and you wake up married, knowing nothing about the person beside you? For all I knew, you could've been some ex-con or someone with the kind of history that could hurt me or my family."

She just shook her head and rolled her eyes, and she didn't answer even though she knew that was childish.

He was slamming his fists against the door when it burst open. She wasn't sure what expression was on her face as she stared at the splintered frame. He was breathing heavy and was now inside the room. His chest…the way he pulled in a breath had her eyes going right there. Did she remember what he was like naked, her hands on his chest, those abs, those arms? Oh yeah, she did.

He stalked toward her like a cat, so controlled, and she could feel the power oozing from him. She pressed her hands to the dresser behind her but didn't pull her gaze from him. His eyes were deep amber, controlled, passionate, strong. She could feel the fire in him, knowing he couldn't be bent. Once he got an idea, he wouldn't change his mind. *Pure male arrogance!*

He was right in front of her, his eyes dipping to her lips, and she had to fight the pull, wanting to feel his hands on her. Would he touch her or walk away? She wanted him to run his hands over her arms, around her back, over her ass, and touch her everywhere, to lower his head and kiss her deeply and mean it instead of doing it as a pretense for the camera.

She squeezed the lip of the dresser, her fingers digging into the wood as she fought the urge to press her hands to the flat of his chest, the soft cotton of his simple gray T-shirt that did little to hide the athlete underneath. His wide chest and broad shoulders exuded a strength that he couldn't pull back. He was so close now that she could smell the hint of sandalwood from the soap he used. She could smell the steak he'd eaten, and his lips were right there.

She dropped her gaze to his lips and felt his hand slide around her back, pulling her hard against him. She heard the squeak that she knew had passed her lips just as he lowered his to hers, kissing her hard, tender, and deep. She could feel every angle of him press into her as her arms, with a mind of their own, looped around his neck. His hand was on her ass, running over the curve, and then he lifted her and had her sitting on the edge of the dresser, her legs around his.

His kiss turned demanding. She tasted him and struggled to breathe, but at the same time she didn't want to break the kiss for air as his hands slid over her back, pressing into her and feeling every inch of her. Then he lifted her, her legs wrapped around his waist, and lowered her to the bed.

This wasn't a simple kiss, not a simple touch: This was passion and emotion and wanting. Yes, she wanted him as he pressed her onto the bed and got on top of her, pushing her into the mattress with all his weight, taking both her hands, her arms, and holding them up above her head. She couldn't move as he kissed her cheek, her neck, and then her chest, right between her breasts.

He ran his hand over both her breasts, over the flat of her stomach, and down. It wasn't a light touch; it was the touch of a man who believed he had every right to touch a woman the way he was, as if she was his—even though, in a way, she was. Did she want him to stop? She thought she'd die if he did. *Please, no. Please don't stop.*

Neither of them said a word. He slid his hands under her shirt and lifted her bra, running his hands over her breasts, both of them, touching, teasing. Her hands found their way to his T-shirt and lifted.

He pulled back and stood up to lift it over his head, and she saw how hard he was. He yanked off her cotton lounging pants and underwear and pulled her up as she slipped off her hoodie and lifted off her shirt, then unfastened her bra. He was already naked, and he lifted her into his arms and started walking.

"Where are we going?" Her voice sounded so odd as

he crossed the hall into his bedroom and dumped her on his bed, then yanked open the bedside table.

"My room, my bed," he said, "and we need these."

He ripped open a condom and covered himself, and she couldn't pull her eyes from him. Did she want this? Hell, yes. She lay back on the bed as he moved onto it, slid his hands under her thighs, and pulled her toward him, wrapping her legs around him as he slid inside her.

She sighed and pulled in a breath as he moved over her, her hands running over his back. She was pulled into his gaze, his eyes, and the complexity, the heat, the wanting as he took her over the edge to that place of magnificence that she'd never expected to have with her husband.

Chapter Twenty-Six

Michael lay on his back, his forearm tossed over his eyes, as he waited for his breathing to return to normal. His heart was still pounding in his chest. He could feel her beside him on the bed, and in that minute of silence, as his reasoning slowly returned, it hit him that this could be one of those awkward moments after meaningless sex. At the same time, he had to remind himself he'd just shagged his wife.

Yeah, that was right—his wife.

Angie was a woman he barely knew, but he realized he couldn't just slip out of bed, get dressed, and say, "Thanks for the fun." This was a first for him.

"You're not saying anything," Angie said. "I'm kind of wondering what that was. You stalked around, showed your caveman side, tossed me down, and screwed me."

He had to lift his arm from his eyes as he took in Angie naked beside him: her perfect breasts, her slim body, and those brilliant blue eyes that were swimming with questions as she lay on her side, facing him.

"So we're being honest, are we?" He sat up and climbed from bed, then stood naked before her, seeing condom wrappers now lying on the floor.

"It's the only way," she said.

He picked up the unused packages and tossed them back in his bedside drawer, then walked into his en suite to toss the used one into the garbage. He could hear rustling and returned to the bedroom to see her stepping into her sweats, the light gray ones that seemed only to complement her light coloring. She had her back to him as she pulled on her bra and fastened it, lifting her tousled long hair, damp and wavy on the ends. Then she reached for her T-shirt and pulled it on, and he just stood there in the doorway, watching her. She was gorgeous and complicated.

"I wanted you," he said. "You aren't a pushover, and there should be some perks to being married."

She turned to him with surprise and shock, he thought, before she laughed and shook her head. "You're really serious," she stated and started across the room to him. She couldn't hide her interest.

"Of course I am, and I'm also not a fool. I can see you enjoyed it. You enjoyed the way I touched you. Even now, the way you're watching me, you want me again." He knew he sounded arrogant, and she pressed the flat of her hand to his bare chest, which was a mistake, because it had him wanting her again.

"Of course," she said. "You're attractive, hot, but sex is just sex and in no way has anything to do with a relationship." She patted his chest and then pulled her hand away, dropping her gaze to his predicament and seeing how much he wanted her. He could've reached out and touched her, taken her, but she stepped back again.

"So this is a relationship, then?" he said.

She stepped away, her hips swaying as she strode one step, two steps to the door and rested her hand on the doorframe, looking back. "I don't know, is it? I guess it depends on what your idea of a relationship is. We live together, we're married, we talk, we share space, and apparently now we have sex—and I'm hungry." She slid her hand over the doorframe, and he wandered over to where he'd kicked off his jeans, his T-shirt. He pulled them on, and she still stood in the doorway, leaning casually, her arms crossed, appearing far more relaxed than she had earlier.

He strode over to her and ran his fingers through his hair, stopping where she lingered. The way she watched him, he felt as if her walls were starting to crumble. He lifted his hand to her cheek, touching it with the back of his fingers. "Well, then I'd say our dinner's getting cold," he said. "Come on."

He followed her back down the stairs, his hand lingering on the small of her back. She sat on the stool, and they ate in companionable silence for a time.

"I would have done the same," she said as she pushed her finished plate away. He had polished off his steak and was digging into his salad, and he wasn't sure what she meant. Maybe she could tell, as he knew his confusion had to show on his face. He was sure it was a smile that teased the corners of her lips.

"The detective, I mean," she said. "I've seen enough, heard enough about guys hooking up with women to take what they have. You asked me to put myself in your shoes. I'd have done the same, find out everything about you, the skeletons in your closet and the problems that could creep out of the woodwork. I would've planned my exit strategy. I presume that was the plan, right? Find out everything about me and figure out the best way to get rid of me." She slid off the bar stool, lifting her plate with the half-eaten steak.

"Seriously, so is this you saying you're not angry anymore?" he said. He didn't know her well enough, and he was stuck on the fact that she was agreeing.

"Oh, I didn't say that, but…" She rested her plate by the sink and then leaned on the island across from him, and he took in her breasts, her face, her eyes, and the teasing that was there. "What I'm saying is you know way more about me, I'm sure, than I'm comfortable with, than anyone does—and there's one problem with that."

Of course, now he was really confused. He took in the way her smile deepened. Her blue eyes flickered with heat. "And that is?" he said as he pushed his plate away and reached for her hand, which she slid over to him. He touched it and let his thumb linger over the diamond he'd bought her.

"Well, it's only fair that I know everything about you."

He took her in and let his gaze linger. "Sounds only fair. So when do we begin?" He pulled her hand and then reached for her other as he leaned closer, just the island between them.

"How about right now?" she said, allowing her eyes to drop to his lips.

He stood up, leaned across the island, and kissed her. When he pulled back, he saw everything she wasn't trying to hide anymore. "You got it," he said. "Any ideas on how we can start?" He linked his fingers with hers and walked around the island, closing the distance between them.

A slow, easy smile touched her lips. "A few, Friessen. Why don't you kiss me? That'll be a great place to start."

The End

Next in the Friessens, don't miss *Anything For You.*

Cat & Xander return in a Friessen Family novella about hurdles in this young couple's relationship.

Anything For You

A BONUS SHORT STORY

Anything For You

Cat & Xander return in a Friessen Family novella about hurdles in this young couple's relationship

Cat and Xander have been living together for years and for Cat it's everything she wants until an unexpected complication changes everything in this couple's relationship.

But for Xander having Cat means she comes with her very opinionated and interfering father Neil who is always sticking his nose into their relationship. Only this time it isn't Xander Neil will be butting heads with when Cat refuses to marry Xander, but his very stubborn daughter whose somehow believes that marriage isn't for her. How far will Xander have to go to convince Cat that marrying him isn't the worst idea ever?

Anything For You

CHAPTER 1

Cat had been unusually quiet as of late, Xander thought. She strode into the bedroom in a cotton tank and pajama shorts, and he was already in bed, waiting for her. Molly, her Labrador hearing dog, was at the foot of the bed, and Sadie, her rescued shepherd cross, was on the floor on a big dog bed. Flee, the speckled gray Great Dane she'd also rescued, was curled up with Sadie, and all the dogs were watching her.

She ran her hand over each of them and signed good night. It was just something she did, no matter how ridiculous it looked to him. They were her dogs, her support, her safety, her everything, and she depended on them as much as they did on her. The bond between them was both deep and strong, and unbreakable.

When she sat, he tapped her shoulder even though she still had her component attached behind her ear. She flicked her eyes his way, the odd shade of blue that was always filled with such mystery.

"You need to do something about Molly," he said. "She can join her sisters on the floor."

She just smiled as she shook her head and then patted the bed, a gesture for Molly to come closer, which she did, scooting up to sit with her paws forward, wagging her tail, which flicked against Xander's leg.

"She been sleeping with me since you got her for me, and I like having her here," Cat said, nuzzling Molly's face with hers. She kissed her head. "You're such a good girl," she said in that baby-talk way. Yeah, she loved her dogs—and so did he, considering they were her ears and kept her safe from everything, the streets, the people. Only now Molly was between him and her on their bed.

"She's a dog," Xander said. "She can go to our feet, or better yet, the floor." He gestured to Molly, snapping his finger and pointing, but she was having none of it from him, as she merely looked from him to Cat. He couldn't remember when it was that she'd started listening to Cat over him. "Traitor," he added.

He took in Cat's smirk, but she nonetheless clapped her hands and gestured to the foot of the bed. Molly moved, and Cat slid into bed beside him and pulled the clip from her honey-gold hair, letting it fall to her shoulders. She leaned in and pressed a kiss to his lips, then went to reach around to take her component off from behind her ear, but he reached out and slid his hand over her wrist to stop her.

"Hey," he said. "You haven't said anything about your brother and Angie. Michael invited us up to one of his games, to stay for the weekend, but you didn't say anything. I told him today we'd get back to him. I think he wants you to meet Angie."

Cat hadn't said a word to him about the invite since Michael had called that afternoon. When he'd asked, she'd only pulled in a breath as if considering something and then walked away. It had been the same since she'd learned what Michael had done, having a drunken birthday celebration in Vegas and waking up married.

"I didn't think you liked Michael," she said, "but now you're conversing with him like you two are best buds or something."

Okay, maybe he'd been a little too vocal on his opinion of her brother, who had always given him the impression of someone who'd had things way too easy: his privileged childhood with a family of means, his career in the pros, and now his carefree lifestyle in the league.

"I helped him out because he's family," Xander said, "but I never said I didn't like Michael. He's your brother. I just think he expects to have everything handed to him and hasn't had to work as hard as everyone else out there. He gets himself in trouble, and…"

"And you think he deserved what happened to him, his drunken marriage." Cat cut him off.

He wasn't sure what to make of her remark or the way she was staring at him now. The Michael and Cat relationship was a minefield that he wasn't sure how to traverse. It was tricky and filled with far too many unexpected triggers.

"Well, he's still married to her, and you've yet to meet her. I didn't say he deserved it. I said that he screwed up big time, and he did. The drinking, the parties, the girls… He's far from a saint, and yeah, in my opinion, he was irresponsible. But then, your dad has always made it too easy for him, done so much. Even with you, he still hovers."

Neil Friessen was always sticking his nose in their relationship, and even after all these years he and Cat had been together, it was a source of contention between them.

"My mom and dad love us, and my dad just wants us to be happy," she said. It wasn't lost on him that she still hadn't answered him about going to Vancouver, visiting her brother and meeting Angie, his wife.

"You're blowing me off again about Michael. Is that a yes or a no? Doesn't matter to me one way or the other, but he is your brother. I'm trying to be supportive here, Cat."

He knew he'd been a bit of a dick, trashing her brother and pointing out all his flaws over and over, but Cat was doing what she did when she was conflicted: She said nothing and busied her hands in folding the sheet over the blanket. Her face gave nothing away, either, so he rolled on his side, propped up on his elbow, allowing his hand to skim over her bare legs, her thighs.

Her hand rested over his, and she flicked her gaze over to him. Ah, there it was in the complexity of her expression. Something was going on.

"Not sure now is the time," she said, "but sometime… yeah, sure."

Boy, that was noncommittal. She shrugged, and he had a feeling this wasn't about Michael—but then, he could be wrong.

"Well, that was really cryptic. You haven't said two words about his situation or about Angie. Are you pissed, not interested, ready to write him off? Like, what? Seriously, come on, Cat."

She finally lifted her hands, pulled back the covers, and scooted from bed. He could see he'd hit a nerve. "Fine, you want to hear it?" she said. "He screwed up big time and maybe got what he deserved. I knew he was far from a saint, the way he partied hard and drank, the way he loved the ladies not for who they were but just as hot chicks he could screw for fun. I could hear the way he joked about it with the guys on his team. They were likely unaware how it sounded, or maybe they didn't even realize I was there. It was all about looks. Even Angie's history, as sordid as it is and the trouble she got into—yes, I heard everything you said about it. Well, now they're staying married not for love but for how it would look in the media, and you're all okay with it?

"Honestly, Xander, I still want to slap him silly. So you know what? Hold off on replying. I'm not a judgemental bitch, but I'm feeling very much that way, and it isn't sitting well with me. I've always been able to shake it off. Michael is Michael, and we were never overly close, even though we were supposed to be. He was always so into his hockey. He lived and breathed it, and he had more of my mom and dad, if you really want to know, with travelling to games every weekend, all the five a.m. practices before school… I always got dragged along.

"Maybe this is probably not the best time to say it," she continued, "but I hate hockey, everything about it! Even though I had to be there because we were a family, every-thing was so focused on Michael. I hated the cold arenas, having to get up early and sit and watch something that was loud and noisy. Do you have any idea what it's like as a deaf person with a cochlear implant to sit in a noisy, echoing arena, as pucks and players slam against the side-boards, with the announcer, the bells, the whistles, the parents and fans…" She stopped talking.

He could see she'd been holding on to a lot about her brother, about their childhood. Why was this all coming out now? "And let me guess," he said. "You never said anything, just went along with it and smiled and pretended everything was fine."

Cat just lifted her hands and let them fall helplessly to her sides. He took in her small breasts under her tank top. She was always so self-conscious of them, and he knew she still hated walking around naked, even though to him she was perfect. "It was always easier," she said, "and—"

"Cat, we've been through this. Your dad has always steamrolled over both of you, and until you tell him what you're thinking and feeling or that he's crossing boundaries, he'll just keep doing it. You not speaking up to your dad has been the main source of your issues with him."

It had been the main source of his issues with Cat, too, when she let her dad overstep boundaries with them.

"I know that, but he's my dad," Cat said. "I love him. I love my parents. It's just…" She was pacing, and the dogs were now watching her as if they were supposed to do something, likely sensing how agitated she was.

"What, Cat? What is it?" He knew it had come out a little too sharp, but she was avoiding something, evading. He knew her well, likely better than she knew herself. It was just something she did when something was bothering her. Instead of talking it out and rehashing it to death like a normal woman who needed to say her piece and then some, what did Cat do but shut down and bottle every single thing up inside her? "Cat," he said again as he sat up, the sheet dropping down.

She flicked her gaze up to him, pulled in a breath, and said, "I'm pregnant."

<hr>

CHAPTER 2

Xander was in his office, talking on his phone, and she took in her three dogs sprawled in the too-small living room of what she still thought of as his house even though she'd been living with him for over six years.

Molly was on the beige tweed sofa, stretched out, Flee was lying on the hardwood floor, and Sadie was on the loveseat. Yes, she babied her dogs, but to her, they were her kids. Fur got on the furniture, but to Cat, it wasn't a big deal.

She poured herself a cup of tea while sitting at the overcrowded kitchen table. It had four chairs, but only two could be used because it was shoved against the wall in the cluttered dining area. The table was her makeshift office when she was home, and she had her laptop open, checking emails, when she noticed her three dogs sit up and knew that Xander had to be coming that way.

Molly and Sadie both jumped down and sat on the floor, knowing they weren't supposed to be on the furniture. Cat leaned back, lifting her damp hair, feeling bloated in her blue jeans, so she'd opted for navy sweatpants and a bulky T-shirt with a hoodie overtop.

Xander strode in, wearing blue jeans, a baggy gray T-shirt, and a five-o'clock shadow. Yup, hot and dangerous was something he was doomed to be. He hesitated a second and then strode past her to the coffeepot to pour himself a cup. To her, it smelled burnt and stale.

"So you want to talk about last night?" he said. "You kind of dropped a little bomb on me, and then that was it. You did the Cat thing and shut the fuck down."

Oops, he sounded a little pissed, but what could she say? The way he reacted had made her pull into herself. The shock on his face had been something she'd never seen before, especially considering that a man like Xander had seen and heard just about everything. Apparently, his girlfriend of six years announcing she was preggers was something he wasn't ready for. Then again, she wasn't exactly over the moon about it, either. Between dogs and babies, she knew which one she'd pick, hands down.

"No, I climbed in bed and went to sleep," she said, knowing he was standing behind her. "I was tired. It was you, your reaction. I know when you want to talk and when you need a minute. You needed a minute, a lot of minutes, so I gave you last night."

He moved into her peripheral, so she slid around on her chair. Was he angry, unhappy, still freaking out? She wasn't sure which one or all, so she just watched him as she lifted her mug of tea and sipped. Thick dark lashes surrounded his deep brown eyes, which were, at times, intense. Right now, there was an edge to them that she hadn't seen before.

"Point taken. So, pregnant, really, you sure?" he said.

She tilted her head. Seriously, what was it with that

question that really annoyed her? "Yup, one hundred percent. Doctor confirmed," she said. She'd befriended the doctors at the clinic beside the community centre where she worked, and just the week before, she'd been in their office for a quick pee on the stick and a congrats, much to her horror.

"So how far along are we?" he said. So there was a *we* now, but still no smile, and she didn't miss the seriousness that wouldn't leave his expression.

"Eight or nine weeks, give or take," she said. She still hadn't considered what this all meant and wondered what was wrong with her, because from the moment she'd found out, instead of being overjoyed, she'd been worried.

Xander just nodded and rested his mug on the tiny counter of the kitchen, which was open to the living room but still too small. Brown, plain, and lacking any type of personality, the house took the term "functional" to a whole new level.

"I can see you're still freaking out about it," she said, "and you likely need more time to…"

He flicked her a pissed-off gaze. His dark eyes could pack a punch when he was ready to argue and make a point, so she just stopped talking and gave him the floor, so to speak. She waited, but he just shook his head and took a few steps out of the kitchen, taking in the dogs, who were looking up at him and wagging. They were so damn happy. How the hell was a baby going to fit with this? Dogs she could do easily, but a baby? This was going to be a problem.

He turned to her. "We should get married."

She was about to laugh when she realized he was serious. "Why?" she said as she slipped her arm over the back of the scraped-up wooden chair. It too was functional but looked like crap. She took in how all three dogs were now on the sofa and loveseat, as Xander had his back to them.

"Because you're pregnant, that's why." The way he leaned in, she could see he was still freaking out a bit.

"Don't be ridiculous. We're not getting married," she said.

He ran his hands over his face with a scrape of whiskers. "Cat, this isn't the time to be all modern-day woman and say let's just live together. It's worked until now, but you're pregnant, so we should get married. It's not really a big deal, anyway." He lifted his hands and then rested them both on his hips. There wasn't anything about Xander that she didn't love—being with him, touching him, loving him, sharing a life with him. He was the love of her life, but at the same time, this was all she'd ever thought this would be.

"Well, if it's not a big deal, then no need to get married," she said. She knew she was pushing all his buttons and he was fighting the urge to shake her, but she also knew that was something he never would do. It was just the kind of thing she could sense with a man.

Xander had always pushed her out of her comfort zone even when she dug her heels in. Without a doubt, he would always be there, but that was no reason to get married.

She stood up as she flipped her laptop closed. "Besides, I need to get to work, so let's table this intriguing discussion on the pros and cons of marriage."

Xander was still standing there, his arms crossed, and by the way he watched her with hard dark eyes, she could tell he wasn't impressed and had more to say, but sometimes he would also just walk away. "Well," he said, "should be interesting when we tell your parents. Wonder how your dad will react?"

This time, she didn't miss the mischief in his expression. He was staring at her, and he took a step closer until he was right in front of her. He slid his finger under her chin and lifted. She was forced to look at him. He'd hit on the one thing that could worry her: good old Dad and his reaction. Her living with Xander had been a source of contention between Cat and Neil for a good many years, and it had been only in the last few that he'd finally stopped bringing it up, asking when they were going to get married, had she come to her senses yet, and seriously, why him?

"So when do you want to tell them? Because I personally want a front-row seat to that show. It will be entertaining to see his reaction." Xander smiled that devilish grin and then leaned in and kissed her as his hand slid around the back of her head. She said nothing, and he stepped back, lifted a brow, and glanced down to her belly. "It would be better to tell your parents before you start showing."

"That still isn't going to get a ring on my finger," she shot right back to him.

He laughed, retrieved his dark stale coffee, and took a swallow. "We'll see," was all he said as he started back to his office.

The dark addition at the back of the house was where private detective Xander Jennings conducted business, took phone calls, conducted meetings, and organized everything to do with spying, watching, and investigating everyone and everything.

Then there were her parents. Candy and Neil would support her decision, whatever it would be, but at the same time, her dad would also try to maneuver her into something she didn't want to do... So really, she realized, it wasn't that he would support her decision and what she wanted but that he would support what he felt should be her decision and what she should want.

Maybe that was why she suddenly felt sick to her stomach.

CHAPTER 3

Xander took in the big house by the ocean, a modest two-story family home with a large kitchen, a separate dining area, a living room and family room, four bedrooms upstairs, and an impressive glassed-in den off the living room. All of this was on five acres of land, and the house alone would have held four of his own home easily. It was a property that did nothing for him. To him, it just meant more rooms to clean.

He always wondered whether Neil Friessen was thumbing his nose at him because of what he had or if he still believed he wasn't good enough for his daughter. It was likely the latter.

He knocked on the front door, then opened it and stepped inside. "Hello?" he called out just as Candy stepped out of the kitchen, her smile wide, her long dark hair the same as when he'd first met her. She was still slender and gorgeous, and she acted as a voice of reason for Cat's father. Actually, Candy was the only one who seemed to be able to rein Neil in.

"Xander, just you? Where's Cat?" she said, and her smile faltered.

He spotted Neil stepping out of his office. He looked at him the same way every time—like a father who didn't like the guy his daughter was dating. "Xander," was all he said, then nodded. Neil was tough, arrogant, smart, and at times Xander enjoyed pushing his buttons. He was far from boring.

"Cat's meeting me here," he said. "She's got things to do at the center, helping a new family get their deaf child lined up with some programming in the community. She said she'd be here just before we eat."

"Great, well, how about a glass of wine or beer while we wait?" Candy said.

Neil just stared at him, unsmiling. So they were still there even after their time together in Vegas, helping out Michael's girl, Angie. Xander had never believed they'd be best buds, anyway. He had to fight the urge to smile as he kicked off his shoes.

"I'll take the beer, just not that lite crap," he said, staring at Neil, who just rolled his eyes and strode into the kitchen.

Candy took in her husband and then dragged her gaze back to him. "I wonder if you two will ever get along," she said.

"We get along fine," Neil replied as he reappeared with a dark beer and extended the can to Xander just the way he liked it. "Right?" he said as if expecting Xander to agree.

He popped the can and took a swallow. "Sure, whatever you say," he said.

Candy lifted her gaze to the ceiling. She was a wonderful woman but was aware of the pissing contest every time he and Neil were together. He just couldn't stop himself from goading Neil, and Neil couldn't stop himself from sticking his nose into Xander's relationship with Cat.

"So when Cat emailed, she said you had news to share," Candy added. What a difference there was between Cat's mother and father. Xander could see how well the news would be received by both. If anything, tonight would have some fireworks that would make it far from a dull evening.

He just laughed. "Yes, but it's Cat's to tell," he added.

Candy and Neil exchanged a glance. He heard the gate and watched as Neil walked over to the window.

"Ah, there she is," he said. Cat was pulling in, driving the red minivan Neil had bought her. He heard a car door. "Ah, Christ almighty, she had to bring all the dogs?"

Another of his favorite things was Neil's obsessive need for cleanliness. He was positive he pulled out the vacuum every time as soon as they left to clean up the trail of dog hair on everything.

Xander said nothing and kept his back to Neil as he did his best not to laugh out loud. "She loves those dogs, and you should be happy. They make sure she can do everything she wants to do safely."

Neil pulled open the front door, dragging his gaze to Xander as Flee, followed by Molly and Sadie, burst inside. Yeah, even Neil couldn't stop himself from running his hand over the dogs' heads.

Definitely all bark.

"Hey, sweetheart." Neil pulled her into a big hug, the same one he always did. Candy was already in the kitchen and had filled up the dog bowls with water.

"Hi, Dad," Cat said, and Xander waited for her to look his way. He could see it there in her expression, which locked on to him: She was dreading the news to share.

Candy strode into the living room with two glasses of

red, walking over to Cat. "Here you go. Xander already has a beer. So tell us this big news! Is it work, some new grant, a project, what?" Candy sounded so excited, and Xander just watched as Cat accepted the wine from her mom. He wondered how far she'd go to avoid this conversation. She glanced his way, and he couldn't keep the smile from tugging at the corners of his lips. He knew he wasn't making this easy for her.

She set the wineglass down on the sofa table, and he could tell by the way she worked her lip that she was going to drag this out to something bordering on painful. "No, nothing like that. Oh, what is that I smell? Is that dinner? Smells great. Chicken, fish…?" she said, not looking his way. She was stalling and she knew it.

"Kabobs, a Greek marinade with rice." Neil slung his arm over Cat's shoulder.

"Just bite the bullet, Cat," Xander said. "Get it over with."

Everyone was looking at him, and the blue in Cat's eyes flashed with a fire he'd seen only a time or two. He didn't miss the confusion on Neil's face as he looked from him to Cat before letting his arm fall away and stepping around so he could see her face.

"Come on, tell them," Xander said, gesturing toward Candy and Neil. He couldn't keep from flashing a smile to her dad, which he knew was pure arrogance, and he listened to her pull in a breath just as Flee raced in and jumped on the sofa.

"Dad, Mom…" she started, then stopped as Neil went to kick the dog off the sofa.

"Cat's pregnant," Xander said.

Neil stilled and faced him, the shock on his face priceless.

"Oh my God! That is so fantastic," Candy said and

hugged Cat, but Neil was looking between them, the dog now ignored. Sadie jumped on the loveseat, and Molly walked back in, her nails clicking on the floor as water dripped from her mouth.

Xander shrugged as he took in Cat, who he could see was pissed off by the look she was giving him.

"So you're pregnant…like, having a baby?" Neil said. Then he walked around the sofa and over to Cat, where he leaned in, hugged her, kissed her cheek, and smiled big and wide.

Yeah, definitely not what he'd expected.

Neil slid his arm around Cat's shoulders and Candy's and then faced him where he stood, holding his can of beer. "So I'm going to be a grandpa? That's great news! So when's the wedding?" he added.

Xander leveled his gaze over to Cat and gestured with his can to her, seeing the expression on her face—puzzled, guarded, cornered. He wondered what she'd say. "You want to tell your dad?" he said, taking in the exchange between Candy and Neil.

"Tell us what?" Candy asked. "Cat, what is it?"

Cat didn't pull her gaze from him. "Well, we're not getting married, and there's one more thing."

"Why not?" Neil said. "Seriously, you two have been living together for, like, five years—"

"Six and a bit, Neil," Candy interrupted. Cat stepped away, and Neil started pacing.

"Whatever," Neil said. "The point is, you've lived together, and now you have a baby on the way. Isn't it time to get serious?"

Xander realized that Neil was looking at him now, not Cat.

"So you get my daughter pregnant and you can't marry her?" Neil said.

Oh, there he went. He had expected this.

"Dad, this isn't on Xander," Cat said. She actually pressed her hand to her dad's chest as he stepped forward. Yeah, he was worked up, and Candy had her hand on his shoulder…what, to stop him from getting in Xander's face?

"Of course it is," Neil said. "He should be marrying you right now. With a baby on the way, he should want to get this done—"

"Dad, stop!" Cat snapped.

He had never heard her talk to her dad like that before, and he found himself wondering what she was going to say.

"Xander put it out there and suggested we get married," she explained, "and I'm the one who said no."

Anything For You

CHAPTER 4

"Well, that went well," Xander said.

Cat was starting to think that he got off on pushing her dad, digging in the screws. Telling her parents she was pregnant hadn't gone anywhere near how she'd expected—not that she'd known how it would shake out. Her dad had been shocked, to say the least, that it was her who wasn't interested in getting married.

"Your sarcasm isn't helping," she said as she watched her dogs running in the open field at her mom and dad's place. There was a lot more space here than at Xander's cramped bungalow, where the fenced backyard was not even big enough to toss a ball around. She glanced up to him as they walked side by side, and she didn't miss the humor that he wasn't trying to hide.

"Hey, I know how your dad is," he said. "I mean, for how long did he ask you outright when I was going to get around to proposing to you? Then there was him asking me what the hell's wrong with me that I can't put a ring on your finger, and my personal favorite, telling you that you can do better."

Yes, her dad had said all that and more, and she knew it was because he wouldn't believe anyone was ever going to be good enough for his daughter. She shrugged as her hand fell into his. It was easy. He whistled, and the dogs came running.

"You do realize he's not going to let it go," Xander said.

Of course she did, but in this, she wasn't going to bend. "You've never brought up marriage, not once, until I told you I was pregnant, and then all of a sudden you toss out the idea of getting married like it's just another decision, like whether I want to go to the movies, or whether I want Greek or Chinese for dinner—and I want to know who my father is, my real father," she finally said.

Xander pulled her to a stop. The expression on his face had gone from teasing to serious. "Your father is in the house back there, Cat."

She knew what he was saying and shook her head. "You know what I mean, Xander. The man who fathered me."

He was shaking his head and looking out at the horizon. "Is this because you're pregnant? You already know that finding him would be hard, if not impossible. You met your birth mom, your brothers. Remember how well that went? Sometimes it's best to just let things lie."

"You don't get it, Xander. It's not just because I'm pregnant—or maybe it is, I don't know, but it's a question that's been there for a while. You seem to forget that my boyfriend is a private investigator and a damn good one."

He wasn't smiling. In fact, the way he was looking at her, she was convinced he was going to say no. "Flattery won't get you anywhere," he said. "I know you, Cat, so what's the real reason you want to find him? You have two of the best parents, and you know how it went before when you sought out your birth mom. You met her, your curiosity was sated, but Neil and Candy's feelings took a back seat."

"So now you're worried about my dad's feelings?" She knew it sounded cruel and went to pull her hand from Xander, but he just held tight.

"Hey, don't be like that. You know damn well your dad and I don't see eye to eye on a lot of things, but when push comes to shove, I know he'll always have your back. So say I find this father, who, let me also point out, doesn't even know you exist. Do you want to meet him? Is that what this is? Then what?"

She could see her dad waving from the house. Dinner was obviously ready. Xander lifted his hand in a wave in return.

"Look, I don't have all the answers," she said, "but what I do know, Xander, is I want to know who he is, to know the history of where I come from. This baby needs to know where they came from. I guess I just can't shake this wanting. Do I want a relationship with him…?" She just shook her head, because Xander was right. She had the most amazing father and mother and wouldn't trade them for anything, but there was just something about genetics and about knowing where she came from. She couldn't help wondering if this was a question everyone who didn't know who their parents were often wondered.

"You sure? Last chance." He was so matter of fact.

"No, I'm not sure, but do it anyway—and, Xander?"

He looked down at her, giving her everything as she rested her hand on his arm, feeling the pull of his triceps. He said nothing as he waited.

She licked her lips and swallowed, taking in her dad, who walked back into the house. The dogs were running in circles and now heading back their way. "Don't say anything to my parents," she said, and she knew he understood, as he inclined his head and reached for her hand, and they started walking back to the house. "Thanks for indulging me," she finally said, and this time she got a smile.

He pulled in a breath. "You know I would do anything for you."

Anything For You

CHAPTER 5

Xander was seated across from Cat at the large dining room table, and the dogs were all lying down just inside the kitchen on the hardwood floor. Where everyone had wine in front of them, Cat had been poured a glass of milk by her dad. Even he had to stifle a laugh, because Cat hated milk. Instead of saying anything, though, she just stared at the glass, looked up at her dad, and then lifted it and sipped.

"You do realize that I've waited for this day for forever," Neil said, "the day I get to walk you down the aisle and give you away to someone deserving?" He flashed Xander a woeful glance.

Xander just smiled, flashing a charming dimple, and took in Cat, who poked at her chicken kabob and shoved a piece in her mouth.

"Dad, we've been through this already," she said. "Xander is it for me, and I'm not getting married." She lifted her gaze to him, and he wondered if she wanted him to step in.

He said nothing, though, as he slipped all the meat and

veggies off the stick and forked a piece of chicken and pepper into his mouth. This was between Cat and her dad, this little tug of war.

"I don't understand why you wouldn't want to get married," Neil said. "Is there a problem going on with you two? You say he's the one you want, but you balk at marrying him. Maybe this thing between you isn't so forever after all."

Cat's fork clattered to her plate, and he didn't have to glance over to Candy to see she was ready to step in. Cat was on edge, and he wondered how much more she'd take before she stepped up and told him to stop.

"Neil, this is between Cat and Xander," Candy said. "You need to stop pushing."

"Thanks, Mom," Cat said.

Xander put all his attention into eating and even reached for a second kabob as he cleaned up his rice.

"But I guess I'm a little surprised, Cat," Candy continued. "I mean, you two really have been together a long time, and your dad and I didn't say anything when you moved in with Xander even though we worried you were jumping into it way too soon. I told your dad this is your choice, but your dad is right: You're having a baby, and it's not as if you two don't know each other, so I have to wonder, is it something we've done that has you hesitating to get married?"

Neil seemed surprised. Cat, though, was looking to Xander, maybe to encourage him to step in and say something. He shrugged and reached for his beer, mainly because he wanted to wait and hear her excuses, but he was also starting to wonder about himself. Did he want to get married? Marriage was never an institution he had aspired to. It was all about a piece of paper, even though he couldn't see himself with anyone but Cat. He was pretty sure Cat didn't see it the same way, though, so that had him wondering what the real reason was.

"Why are you and Dad pushing so hard for me and Xander to get married?" Cat glanced from her mom to her dad, and he could see the irritation.

"Cat, it's not about pushing," Candy said. "You're not giving us an answer, you're evading, and you think I don't know there's something more going on?" She hesitated and glanced over to Xander as if she was about to say something that would upset him. "Xander, maybe you can shed some light?"

He just shrugged again and chewed, then swallowed, taking his time to consider what he should say. "Well, I guess I would kind of like to know the same thing. You already know how I feel, Cat. I love you. There's no one else. You're the love of my life, and there's nothing easy or unforgettable about you."

She looked surprised, as if this was the first time she'd heard this, even though it wasn't. "Xander, I know how you feel about marriage," she said, then rested her forearms on the table, holding her fork and knife in each hand. "I've heard you, especially when you get one of those cases where someone cheats on a spouse, and you comment on the divorce rate and how expensive marriage is, that it's cheaper and easier to just stay single."

Had he said all that? Of course, and more, considering the trust issues he had. In his investigations, he always wondered when it was that everything went bad in a marriage—after two years with some, ten for others. "That's just work, Cat," he said. "It's just venting and has nothing to do with this."

The way she lifted her brows and her blue eyes flickered, she seemed ready to call him out. He knew she'd taken all the worst he'd seen in other people's crumbling marriages and the venting he'd done and evidently come to the conclusion that he hated marriage.

"I don't dislike marriage, Cat," he continued. He could feel Neil and Candy watching him and wondered if they wanted to add their two cents. All the while, he couldn't pull his gaze from Cat. "It's just that I've seen the worst that can happen when it falls apart and how badly both sides behave. I never said that would be us."

She jabbed her fork toward him. "Xander, that is bullshit and you know it. Are you denying saying people shouldn't get married until after the honeymoon phase has long passed, that if everyone decided to stop getting married, it would put all those slimy divorce lawyers out of business, and kids wouldn't starve and go hungry or homeless while their parents fight about who gets who? And then there's my personal favorite, when you asked what idiot would toss away a good twenty grand for a party that causes a ridiculous amount of stress for everyone involved when that money could be put to better use."

He didn't have to look Neil's way to know he was giving all his attention to him. He was trying to remember when he'd said that and what case he'd been working on. Was this why she didn't want to get married? He set his fork and knife down and reached for the napkin to wipe his hands, then slid back his chair and stood up, taking in the alarm on Cat's face.

"What are you doing?" she said. He could hear the unease in her voice.

He said nothing as he stepped around the table, digging into each step as he walked around Neil, who set down his fork with a clatter. He knew they were wondering what he was doing, and when he stopped beside Cat, he took in the shock and surprise that was staring up at him.

"Cat," he said, "I've seen couples who supposedly love each other do some pretty shitty things, so I've tossed out some thoughtless remarks—but that's all they were." He reached down for her hand and then went down on one knee. Her face paled, and he heard Candy gasp. "Cat, those words were just me venting about a job, and yes, I think weddings can be way over the top, but out of all that, I never in any way meant to insinuate that would be us. You're right that I've never seen marriage as necessary, but I'm also not opposed to it. I love you, you're having my kid, and if you have any doubt that I'm serious about getting married, please get that out of your head, because I think you know me well enough to know that I don't do anything unless I'm committed. Cat, I'm down on one knee, and I'd really like to get up, because this hardwood is damn uncomfortable, but I'll stay here until you say you'll marry me."

She was staring at him, her mouth open, and he still had her hand in his. He could see she was trying to make sense of this marriage proposal and that he was doing a piss-poor job of trying to convince her.

"Seriously, Cat, I'm getting a cramp in my knee. I don't have a ring, but, damn, I'll get one. I'll get you the biggest—"

She held up her fingers and signed otherwise.

"Okay, the tiniest diamond ring," he said, "so small people will have to use a magnifying glass to see that it's real. Seriously, Cat, you came into my life and turned me upside down. I'm never alone with you, and you make me a better man—even though it would be nice to not have to share our bed with the dogs, but I do it because, damn, I can't live without you."

"Cat…" her dad said. Candy just cleared her throat, maybe so Neil would stop.

Cat glanced over to her mom and then her dad and back to him. "You're serious?" she asked.

He crossed an X over his heart. "Completely. Do you think I'd be humbling myself on my knees with your dad here otherwise?" He thought he heard Neil swear, and Cat couldn't suppress the smile that touched her lips as she seemed to consider it.

"All right," she said. "I'll marry you."

"Yay!" Candy clapped her hands and scooted back her chair as Xander stood up, feeling Neil pat his shoulder. Candy hugged Cat, and Neil was standing before him, appearing very much the proud father with a lot on his mind.

"Great," Neil said. "Now that that's solved, let's talk about the wedding."

This time, he heard Candy groan behind him, and he lifted a brow, taking in Neil, knowing that he was very much the kind of man who would turn his daughter's wedding into a three-ring circus.

CHAPTER 6

Xander had found her father, or one of three possible fathers.

All had been stationed down in the Cancun area. The man in question was still in the military, based overseas in Germany, currently in counterintelligence. Of the other two, one had died in a knife fight in a bar parking lot in Luxembourg, just two drunks, too much liquor, and no sense. The third had gotten married, with four kids, but had struggled with drinking and subsequently lost his family and was now a used car salesman in Des Moines, driving a beater and living in a basement suite, delinquent on his child support payments.

He knew he needed to give Cat a choice, but at the same time, he knew that if Neil found out, he'd become seriously unglued. This was just one of those things he wouldn't handle well—which was why he found himself outside on her parents' back deck in the summer sun, alone while he listened to the sounds of the family inside: Michael, Angie, Cat, Neil, and Candy.

The patio door slid open, and Neil stepped out.

Xander turned to see him, and Neil looked right and then left, then took a step and another over to him. He was dressed in deep blue jeans and a Canucks jersey, the proud father of a hockey star.

"So you've snuck off out here alone," Neil said as he leaned on the rail not far from him.

"I'm not alone. I'm watching the dogs," Xander stated.

Neil didn't look his way but shared the space, looking out at the dogs running and playing as if that was everything to see. "So Cat told me she asked you to search out her biological father."

He never would've seen that coming. He squeezed his can of beer, which was getting a little warm, and took in Cat through the screen door. She now sported a small baby bump in a pair of jean shorts and a deep red T-shirt, and she was laughing with Michael, Angie, and Candy.

"Yeah," he finally replied. "So is this where you tell me not to do it?"

Neil's face flashed an odd expression as he leaned on the rail and then turned his full gaze to him. It wasn't happy or pissed off; it was something that seemed resigned. He shook his head. "Nope. As my wife has pointed out to me, my kids are grownups and have to run their own lives, fix their own problems, make their own choices."

It wasn't much of an answer, but at least it was something. At the same time, it wasn't what he'd expected. "So what did you want to do?" Xander said. "Because I found him—or one of three possibilities."

Neil raised his brows, surprised, and then shifted his gaze back out to the horizon, the dogs, the property, the ocean view, but he was likely seeing none of it.

"I'm good," Xander said, knowing he sounded arrogant. "You already know that."

"Any red flags, problems?" Neil asked.

What could he say? "Likely, maybe," he replied and shrugged, then took a swallow of his beer.

Neil nodded and stood straighter as the screen slid open, and Cat stepped out along with Michael and Angie, who were still married and appeared to be in the honeymoon phase, all chemistry. He wondered if it would last.

Neil stepped in closer and said to him, "Tell her, but I don't want her hurt, so I'm trusting you to make sure she's looked after, to see that this doesn't become an issue." He held out his hand, and Xander shook it for the first time, squeezing hard.

Cat stepped closer. "So what are you two talking about?" she asked. He didn't miss the suspicion in her eyes.

"Xander has something to tell you, and since you both denied me that big wedding I wanted to give you, I have a surprise for you," Neil said.

Of course Neil was choked about it, but Xander had been relieved at having a small wedding, just family in the backyard, the week before. Cat slid her hand into his as Neil disappeared into the house, then came back out a minute later with an envelope.

Xander wasn't sure what to say, what to expect. Cat gave him a puzzled glance and shrugged as Neil called everyone over.

"So I told you that I had something for you at that ridiculously small wedding—which didn't even have a decent aisle for me to walk you down. Well, here it is." Neil held out an envelope, and Cat took it.

She looked up to him, her expression amused, before she opened the envelope and pulled out title papers for a house. "Dad, you bought us a house?" Cat said.

Xander had to look again, seeing the address and knowing it was only a block away, a nice area. He wasn't sure what to say.

"Seriously?" Cat said, and he was stuck on how happy she sounded. "Wow, this is great."

"I did," Neil said, "around the corner, a decent place with room for the dogs to run, and with my grandchild on the way, your small..." Neil hesitated, and Xander knew he was likely fighting the urge to say *dump*, the word he used to describe his house every time he saw him. "Well, let's just say you need room, you need to be closer, and I'm not taking no for an answer. "

"Thanks, Dad." Cat strode over to Neil and hugged him, then her mom, and Xander took in the amused expression on her brother's face.

"Cat, that's just a Dad thing," Michael said. "Just wait —he'll furnish it for you, too."

Neil made a face, and Candy said something to Michael. Cat walked back over to him, holding the papers and looking happier than he'd ever seen her.

"So you want this...house?" he said.

She flicked her gaze up to him and then past him. "Yeah, I do. The dogs need room, I need room, and the baby is going to need room so I'm not tripping over everything."

He couldn't keep the smile from touching his lips. "For you, I'll give," he said, and she poked his chest.

"Hey, my dad said you have something to tell me," she said. She was looking hopeful, and he flicked his gaze over to Michael and Angie, to Neil and Candy, her parents, who would do anything for her and Michael. They were the kind of parents who were meant to be parents.

He glanced down to her again. "I found your biological father," he said.

She touched her chest with surprise and shock. "And...?"

He flicked his gaze over to Neil, who was watching

them from where he stood with his arm around Candy. "Sorry, babe," he finally said. "He died."

She nodded once and then flicked her gaze up to him. "Well, thanks for looking. Is there any other family, wife, kids, anyone?"

He just shook his head. "Nope, he was in a drunken fight, nothing that ended well. But see over there?" He gestured to Neil. "He's the only father you'll ever need."

Cat looked from Neil to him and raised her brow. "I know that," she said. "He's overprotective, hovering, and—"

"And he would do anything for you, just like I would," he said, then leaned down and kissed her.

"I love you, Mister Jennings," Cat said and looped her arms around his shoulders as he pulled her closer.

"I love you, Missus Jennings," he replied.

He took in her beautiful smile as the dogs made their way up on the deck and bumped against him and Cat and everyone. Okay, he had to admit that maybe a bigger house with an actual yard would be a good thing, and as he pulled Cat into his arms, he wondered by the way Neil watched him whether he had any idea what he'd done. Maybe. He was aware that lying to Cat was exactly what Neil would have done, too. He'd be damned if he'd allow anyone to mess with Cat or his family.

There was one thing about Cat. She might have seemed helpless and timid, but that was a facade for those who didn't really know her. She was smart, amazing, stronger than everyone gave her credit for, and she never let him steamroll over her. She was the strongest, most difficult, most complex woman, and while at times she allowed fear to get in her way, she always faced it better than anyone he'd ever met. He'd read enough about the two men who were still alive to know there was no way in hell he'd allow either of them anywhere near his wife.

Cat nudged him. "What are you thinking about?"

He took her in and smiled. "Just how lucky I am to have you."

Turn the page for a sneak peek of
THE HOMECOMING the next book in THE FRIESSENS
Available in print, eBook & coming soon to audio

The Homecoming

The Homecoming is a special request from one of my long-time fans, who asked for a book that would revisit the entire Friessen clan with a reunion so you can catch up with all of the family, their wives, and their children. I just couldn't say no to that. I mean, what could be better than a new book featuring all your favorite Friessen characters and the new generation that has begun?

> When the ever expanding Friessen clan gets together for a family reunion, what they think will be a peaceful time away turns into a nightmare.
>
> Susan H.

> Several of our favourite characters are put in danger and a serious secret is revealed by someone you'd never suspect.
>
> Patti B.

Catch up with your favorite family, the Friessens, as four generations come together for what they anticipate to be a fun-filled weekend with babies and children, loads of love, and laughter. You can expect all the drama of young love, from the secrets to the hidden truths in a seemingly perfect marriage.

However, one fateful moment changes everything in this unforgettable story. When three lives are put in danger, the fallout could ultimately shatter the deep love and trust in this family, dividing them forever—and the cost could be something far greater than any of them could have imagined.

The Homecoming

CHAPTER 1

"So what was that about?" Emily asked, appearing tired. They had just travelled six hours on a cramped over-booked flight from Seattle that had been delayed by nearly ninety minutes. She yawned and swept her fingers through her shoulder-length brown hair, which was slowly becoming lighter from the highlights she kept adding to hide the spots of gray.

Brad glanced at his Android before tucking it in the back pocket of his jeans and taking in the conveyor belt at the Cancun airport. On it were a single black suitcase and two boxes tied together. Not one of the bags from their flight had been unloaded, and they had been standing there for nearly ten minutes. He was still puzzled by the message his dad had left.

"I don't know," he said. "Weird, is all—something about whether I could call him back to confirm who all is coming to stay with them…"

Did Rodney mean for the next weekend? He'd give it another listen, as it made no sense. The entire family was travelling there, all the kids and grandkids, to stay at the

Cancun resort together for the first time. They had even booked rooms in the same wing. Jed and Diana and their brood were also on the way, as were Andy and Laura and theirs. His mom and dad knew that was the plan.

He was starting to wonder if his dad was becoming more forgetful. It wasn't like him to leave that kind of scatterbrained message. He rolled his shoulders, feeling restless after having to sit for so long and feeling the angst of his family around him, their ups and downs, the bickering of Becky and Tom.

"Maybe we should swing over to the house first before we check in, make sure everything's good," Brad said.

Emily's jaw slackened, and he wasn't sure what she was about to say.

"Have you seen Neil?" Candy said, appearing beside him, her long dark hair freshly cut to shoulder length.

He spotted Xander and Cat also walking their way. Xander had a deep brooding look and a perpetual five o'clock shadow, his jeans riding low with a swagger. He held Cat's hand, and she appeared lost in thought. Brad was still stuck on the sight of her new hair, red with dark lowlights.

"No, I haven't, not since we got off the plane," he said. "Trevor!" he called out and waved, seeing his son was holding Jasmine's hand, pressed against a concrete wall.

Trevor began pulling her along over to them, and what was she doing but holding her hand over her eyes, following him blindly? Of course, a number of odd looks were passed their way. The Cancun airport was crowded and chaotic, and he'd forgotten how loud and noisy it was, concrete and old.

Something seemed to be up, a strangeness, an energy he couldn't put his finger on—or maybe it had just been too long since he'd been there. They were all feeling the heightened sense of worry, stress, or expectation, and likely the restlessness of having travelled all day, too, not to mention the fact that they were all still dressed for the Seattle rain. Maybe some time to decompress by the pool with a beer, catching up with his family, would definitely help. Yeah, he couldn't wait.

"Mom, can you take Gilly?" Becky said. "Tom's on the phone again, and I have to go to the bathroom." She was wearing a ratty old oversized T-shirt and dark-rimmed glasses, with deep circles under her eyes, and her hair was pulled up in a really messy bun. He'd never expected to see this kind of harried expression on her face. His grand-daughter, Gilly, was crying and kicking to get down, her nose running and her blue eyes filled with tears. She was fast coming up on the terrible twos.

"Here, come to Gramps," he said and reached for her, immediately feeling her soaked-through diaper under her floral dress, which was riding up. She was barefoot like she always was. "She's wet, Becky—and where is Tom?"

Emily patted Gilly's back, and she whimpered, staring up at him and tossing her head back. Becky wasn't the greatest at changing the baby's diapers, and Gilly, he swore, had the mischief of all his kids combined in one. Becky just lifted her hand and let out a frustrated sigh. He could see her patience was wearing thin.

"Over there, on the phone. Some hospital emergency, he said. Don't know why he's insisted on calling back. Family holiday means just that, a holiday, with no work, not sticking me with everything." Becky actually slipped the diaper bag off her shoulder, and for a second he thought she'd dump it on the ground, but Emily grabbed it. He took in Cat, who was now talking to Candy. Both also seemed on edge as they looked around.

"Dad, where're our suitcases?" Trevor asked. Jasmine was making a weird noise with her mouth.

"Be patient," Brad said. "They'll be here soon."

Becky was already walking toward the bathroom when Fletcher, Jack, Katy, and Steven appeared. He could smell an odor and knew it was Gilly.

"Okay, you can't wait. You need changed now," Brad said as he held out his granddaughter, then spotted the luggage after hearing the thump of the first suitcase dumping down the conveyor belt. "You need to talk to your daughter about taking better care of Gilly," he said.

Emily frowned and shook her head. "Hey, just as easy for you to have a talk with her, as well. Come on, Gilly. Grandma will change your diaper."

Brad passed Gilly over just as Candy tapped his arm.

"I still can't find Neil," she said. He wasn't sure what to make of her expression—off, anxious. Over what, he didn't know.

"Well, I'm sure he couldn't have gone far…" he started to say just as he spotted his brother walking toward them with Cat and Xander's baby boy tucked into a baby carrier strapped across his chest. He looked ridiculous and happy in Bermuda shorts and sandals, working a piece of gum. This casual, laid-back Neil was a lot to get used to.

"Dad, where were you?" Cat said. "You can't keep taking off with the baby…" She reached for baby Nathan, who was the spitting image of Xander, with big eyes, thick dark lashes, and the same intense expression. He was unbelievably quiet, easy, the exact opposite of Gilly.

"No one thought to grab the bags?" Neil said. "Thought we'd be out of here." He was still wearing the carrier and had a diaper bag over his shoulder. "And you can thank me, Cat. I changed the baby. He's hungry, too."

Over by the conveyer, Katy was saying something to

Trevor, and Steven was pulling a luggage cart over and grabbing luggage off. While it was great having a son-in-law to take care of things for him, Brad figured he should help.

"So I had a message from Dad," he said. "I think I'll swing by the house first before the resort. He seemed under the impression we're all coming next week and that we're staying there?"

Neil gave him the oddest look and then just shook his head. "Seriously?" he said. "Well, if you are, bring them back with you to the resort. I'm sure Diana, Jed, and their crew are already there. Andy, too, I think. I got a text from him that they arrived earlier today. I would've thought Jed or Andy would call them." Neil pulled his iPhone from his pocket and scanned his messages.

Brad then spotted Xander, who had a second luggage cart, over by Steven. The two of them were handling, talking, giving Jack and Fletcher orders, and tossing bags onto the luggage carts. He gestured with his chin. "You think they got everything?"

Neil laughed softly. "Hope so. One of the benefits, I'd think, of having to put up with a son-in-law. Let them get it."

Emily and Becky were walking back side by side, Emily holding Gilly on her hip. His daughter appeared far from put together, but at least Tom was off his call and was now over by Steven, tossing a bag on one of the carts.

"Dad, Jasmine needs to go," Trevor called out. Jasmine was now standing close to him, staring at the ground and moving side to side. She was over-stimulated, over-everything.

"Katy, take Trevor and Jasmine and start heading through customs," he said, but just then, Steven headed over, pushing one of the luggage carts, and he gestured with his thumb to Brad and said, "We got all the bags. Let's go."

Neil's phone dinged, and his expression changed as he stared at the screen.

"What is it?" Brad asked.

Neil shook his head. Everyone was talking and following Steven, Xander, and the carts to the final check point. "Not sure… A text from Andy. He asked if we've heard from Mom and Dad."

Candy was pulling on his arm, saying something, and he just shook his head. Emily, Becky, and Tom were now standing there, staring at them as if they'd just figured out something was up.

"You know what?" Neil said. "Maybe I'll join you and stop in at Mom and Dad's."

"What, why? What's going on?" Becky piped in. Tom scooped Gilly into his arms and kissed her cheek.

"Nothing, most likely, but…you talk to your grandma?" Brad said. He knew Becky talked more with his mom than anyone else in the family.

Becky pushed the bridge of her glasses up her nose and shrugged. "Not since yesterday. Why, what's up?" She was looking from him to Neil, and so were Emily and Candy, too.

"Just a message from your grandpa. Seems like he thinks we're not coming until next week and that we're staying there. So I think Neil and I will swing by there first. You all go on to the resort and get checked in."

Becky never blinked and then slowly turned to Neil. "That's ridiculous," she said. "They know we're coming today. Grandma and I are booked in for a pedicure after dinner tonight at the resort. If you're going to drop in on Gram and Gramps, then I'm coming, too."

Tom just shook his head and walked away.

"You should go to the hotel with your husband, Becky, and your daughter," Brad said, but what did his daughter do but shake her head? She was pure stubbornness.

"No, I'm going with you," she said. "Besides, I want a minute aside to talk to Grams without everyone there and without Tom passing Gilly off to me."

Then Becky was walking off, and Emily levelled a hard look his way, which he knew well meant he needed to do something about their daughter. That left four: Candy, Neil, Emily, and him.

"Do you think if we hang back here for a second, they'll forget we're here?" Neil said just as Candy tapped his chest.

"Oh, stop it," she said. "Why don't we let the rest of them head on to the resort, and the four of us can stop in and see your parents?" She lifted her chin to where the Mexican security agents were looking through the largest black suitcase. "And Becky," she added as an afterthought, likely because she knew well how stubborn his daughter was.

Brad looked over to where Katy and Steven were herding Jack, Fletcher, Trevor, and Jasmine through the checkpoint. Then there were Tom and Becky and Gilly, Cat and Xander and Nathan, and as they all passed through, he couldn't see them anymore.

This was meant to be a fun-filled reunion, but it seemed something else was brewing in the wind that he couldn't put his finger on.

The Homecoming

CHAPTER 2

"Neil, who are you texting now?" Candy said.

He could see the three dots that meant Xander was considering how to answer his last text: a long thinking pause, then no response. "Just making sure Cat has everything she needs for Nathan. I asked the manager to make sure there's a crib, fresh cotton blankets, nothing synthetic, plenty of drinking water…"

He glanced up, taking in the shock on Emily and Candy's faces. Brad raised his brows—mocking him, he was sure. Becky didn't seem too interested from where she sat beside Candy in the limo, looking out the window, lost in thought. He was still staring at a blank screen, about to send a second text to Xander, when Candy took his phone from his hands and powered it off.

"You're being ridiculous and overstepping again," she said. "Leave them alone. Seriously, Neil, this over-the-top obsessive need of yours has got to stop. Xander can look after them. The baby is fine."

Brad said nothing but appeared close to laughing at

him, and he watched as his wife tucked his phone in her purse.

"Hey, he's my grandson," Neil said. "I just want to make sure he has everything he needs…" And he wanted to make sure Cat was comfortable, too, because the dogs weren't there to help her. He just couldn't shake the need to be close to his grandson and worry about anything and everything that could go wrong.

This time, Brad was laughing and shaking his head. "Just admit it, Neil. You won't be happy until you have everyone living under your roof. Just get a bigger house so you can stick your nose into their business all the time. Oh, wait! You're over at Cat's almost every day now, and you even have Nathan stay over at your place how often…?"

"Well, at least Uncle Neil cares," Becky spoke up.

The shock and surprise on everyone's face mirrored his, he thought, as they took the turnoff to his parents' estate, up the long driveway lined by trees that had grown back. He'd never heard her speak that way, and he took in Emily's expression as she lifted her hand, at a loss.

"Becky, are you kidding me? What's going on with you?" she said.

"Nothing, sorry. Shouldn't have said anything." Becky lifted her hand to wave it off, and he could feel how on edge she was. Even Candy tossed him an uneasy look. Brad was levelling that shrewd gaze on her, the tough-love one he'd seen a time or two when the kids were growing up.

"What is this about, Becky? You don't get to play that game, saying we don't care and then never mind. You're a grown woman, a mother…" Brad didn't pull his gaze away, but Becky was stubborn—just like Brad in so many ways. Neil wondered who'd blink first.

"Are you needing a break with the baby? Is that what

this is?" Emily finally broke the standoff. He wanted to reach out and tell her to stop, especially the way she was looking imploringly at Becky, always trying to make it easier.

"Well, I kind of have one now because I didn't give Tom a choice, right?" she said.

Even to Neil, that didn't sound like Becky. He found himself leaning forward to see the stubborn set of her jaw, the way she glanced from Brad to Emily and then back to the estate.

They pulled up and parked, but he thought Brad might still have another thing or two to say. Instead, Becky had the door open and was stepping out. Brad just shook his head, and Neil raised a brow, wondering what that was all about. He'd missed something big going on between Becky and Tom. Trouble? Maybe.

"Care to share what the issue is?" Neil asked as the four of them remained in the back. The driver was now out of the vehicle, and Becky was heading across the circular driveway, nearly to the front door.

Brad just shook his head, "Mood swings?" he said. "I don't know, but she's really pushing with Tom, and you know I'm not a fan of his."

Emily made a rude noise he'd never heard before and stepped out, and Candy followed.

"So is it work, or not working?" Neil said. "Is there trouble, she wants to leave him…what?"

Brad just shook his head and climbed out. Neil took his time, taking in his brother as he handed a cash tip to the driver. Candy and Emily were already walking to the house.

"It's locked," Becky called out, then rapped the brass knocker on the front door and pressed the bell. He could hear the chime from outside.

"Maybe Mom and Dad are at the resort?" Neil said. "But Maria and Carlos should still be here."

"They don't work here anymore," Becky said.

Candy tried to open the door, but it was locked, and she tossed Neil an uneasy gaze. Brad was over at the huge window to the sunken living room.

"Drapes are pulled. Can't see in," he said, then tapped on the window, but they didn't hear anything.

"Since when are Maria and Carlos not here?" Neil said. The look Candy gave him showed it was the first she was hearing of it, too.

Becky just shrugged. He took in how not put together she was, in her faded oversized shirt and baggy ultra-worn jeans, wearing flip flops. The glasses were new, too. He wondered if she'd bothered to brush her hair before pulling it up in a messy bun.

The limo was already pulling away when Brad shoved his fingers in his mouth and whistled. The driver should have stopped, but he kept going down the driveway and was gone around the bend, the trees blocking them from view.

"Let's walk around back. Maybe they're out at the pool," Brad said.

"Or not here," Candy suggested. "Neil, don't you have a key still?"

Neil walked around the house, taking in the empty driveway that led to the garage in back. He jammed his hands in his pockets, but his keys weren't there. They were tucked in his bags, on their way to the resort. "Not with me," he tossed out over his shoulder.

Brad was close behind him, his cowboy boots scraping against the walkway. He wore blue jeans and a deep blue T-shirt, but at least it was short sleeved. His hair was now a mix of dark and white. He squinted in the bright sun and pulled his phone from his pocket, then texted something and shook his head. "Jed and Andy are at the pool," he said. "Haven't seen Mom and Dad."

They took in the back of the house. The pool still had the vinyl cover over it, and the patio furniture was in the same place he remembered. The umbrella was down as if his mom and dad hadn't been out that day.

"Mom, Dad!" Brad cupped his hands and called out. He was loud, and Neil expected to hear something. He reached for the back door that led into the kitchen to find that it was locked, and Brad walked over to the double doors off the dining room and tried the knob, both of them. Locked. He just shook his head.

"Well, this is really strange," Neil said, taking in Candy, Emily, and Becky, who had her arms crossed over her breasts. She was far from the happy girl he'd known. When had she slipped into this?

"Well, maybe you should call the resort, get a car out here for us," Brad said.

Neil held his hand out to Candy. "Can I have my phone?"

Just then, there was the click of a lock, and the door opened. Neil took in the dark eyes and dark hair of the man who had answered—in his early fifties, maybe. "Can I help you?" he said in a deep voice, a southern accent that was more a twang than a drawl.

Neil laughed, only it wasn't a laugh, because this was ridiculous. "Yeah, who are you?" he said. "Where are my parents, Rodney and Becky Friessen?"

The man was tall, broad shouldered, in a ratty T-shirt and jeans, with a scar at his jawline. "I work here, manage the estate. Who are you?" The man looked at him and then dragged his gaze over to Brad, and it wasn't lost on him that he was standing in the doorway, blocking it as if they were unwelcome guests.

"Are my mom and dad here, Becky and Rodney?" Brad said.

The man took in Brad as if he suspected he would cause trouble, then pulled his gaze back to Neil, who expected him to step back and let them in, but he didn't. The unease he'd been feeling earlier now felt more like a vise, squeezing all the air out of his chest.

"Nope," the man said and made a face, and Neil thought he was going to close the door on them.

"Look," he said. "We're family. I'm Neil, and that's my brother Brad. Our wives are over there, and my niece. Surely my parents said to expect us?" He wondered if maybe Jed was behind this—a joke, maybe. He found himself trying to see past the man when he felt a hand slam into his chest to stop him.

"All I can say is they're not here," the man said, "and they said nothing about family coming. If you don't mind, I'd rather not take chances. This is private property. You're trespassing, and I'm tasked with looking after this property and all. There have been break-ins, a lot over the last while, men breaking in and living in empty homes, taking them over, so if it's all the same to you…" He didn't smile. He had a kind of hardness that let Neil know they weren't getting past him.

The phone was ringing inside, and Neil glanced over to see Brad with his cell phone to his ear. The man only glanced once over his shoulder, and he was tempted to push past. This was crazy, ridiculous.

"Well, see here," Brad said. "We're not leaving, and you haven't answered us about our parents. Where are they? That's me calling." He held his cell phone up and then ended the call as if proving a point, as the ringing stopped inside. "What is your name?"

Neil wondered when it was that Maria and Carlos had left and where his parents had found someone like this.

"Davis," the man replied. "Now, as I said…"

"Davis, great," Brad interrupted. "There seems to have been a miscommunication somewhere. I appreciate this vigilance and you taking your job seriously, protecting this estate, but I'm sure if you get my mom and dad on the phone, they'll tell you…" A phone was ringing inside again, quieter this time, and Brad was holding up his cell. "That would be me calling my dad's cell phone. So, again, where are my parents?"

It happened so fast.

Davis reached behind his back, and there was a gun. He flicked the safety and pointed it straight out to the women.

Neil stepped back, his hands up, hearing a gasp and shriek—Candy or maybe Emily. It was so precise, Davis's stance, his familiarity with the gun. Neil could always tell when someone lived and breathed guns, knew how to hold and use them. The man appeared to be one with the weapon.

"Whoa, whoa! What is this? Let's just keep it together, here," Neil said.

Davis held the gun, aiming as if he knew what he was doing. He didn't even glance his way as he jabbed his right hand to Neil. "Take a step back, both of you, because right now I have the babe in the glasses in my sights, and I never miss. So back the fuck up. There's no second chance. I ask you to do something once, and the next time I pull the trigger."

"Okay, just relax," Brad said. "Here, put the gun on me, not my daughter."

Neil couldn't pull his eyes away from the threat to his family. He was the one standing between them, and Brad took a step away from the house, over to the women. He couldn't believe this was happening. Where were his mom and dad?

He dared to glance only once behind him to Candy, Emily, and Becky knowing the shock on their faces did little to help this situation. Like, what the hell was going on here? His mom and dad, were they inside? Were they hurt? They weren't answering. Candy, Emily, Becky, and Brad… they were all in deep shit.

He went to reach out to Candy when he heard the distinct sound of a gun being cocked, a sound that chilled him to the bone.

"You two don't listen, do you?" Davis said. Then the gun fired with a pop.

He heard a scream, long and loud, and Brad roared.

Davis flicked the gun over to him. "Why is it that everyone has to make everything so damn hard? I told you I'd only say it once. If you just listened and did as you were told, I wouldn't have shot her."

About the Author

With flawed strong characters, characters you can relate to, New York Times & USA Today Bestselling Author Lorhainne Eckhart writes the kind of books she wants to read. She is frequently a Top 100 bestselling author in multiple genres, and her second book ever published, The Forgotten Child, is no exception. With close to 900 reviews on Amazon, translated into German and French, this book was such a hit that the long running Friessen Family series was born. Now with over 100 books and multiple series under her belt her big family romance series are loved by fans worldwide. A recipient of the 2013, 2015 and 2016 Readers' Favorite Award for Suspense and Romance, Lorhainne lives on the sunny west-coast Gulf Island of Salt Spring Island, is the mother of three, her oldest has autism and she is an advocate for never giving up on your dreams.

Lorhainne loves to hear from her readers! You can connect with me at:
www.LorhainneEckhart.com

lorhainneeckhart.le@gmail.com

The Bloodline (Andy & Laura)
The Promise (Diana & Jed)
The Business Plan (Neil & Candy)
The Decision (Brad & Emily)
First Love (Katy)
Family First
Leave the Light On
In the Moment
In the Family
In the Silence
In the Charm
Unexpected Consequences
It Was Always You
The First Time I Saw You
Welcome to My Arms
Welcome to Boston
I'll Always Love You
Ground Rules
A Reason to Breathe
You Are My Everything
Anything For You
The Homecoming
Stay Away From My Daughter
The Bad Boy
A Place of Our Own
The Visitor
All About Devon
Long Past Dawn
How to Heal a Heart

The McCabe Brothers
Don't Stop Me (Vic)
Don't Catch Me (Chase)
Don't Run From Me (Aaron)

Don't Hide From Me (Luc)
Don't Leave Me (Claudia)
Out of Time (John)

The O'Connells

The Neighbor
The Third Call
The Secret Husband
The Quiet Day

The Wilde Brothers

The One (Joe and Margaret)
The Honeymoon, A Wilde Brothers Short
Friendly Fire (Logan and Julia)
Not Quite Married, A Wilde Brothers Short
A Matter of Trust (Ben and Carrie)
The Reckoning, A Wilde Brothers Christmas
Traded (Jake)
Unforgiven (Samuel)
The Holiday Bride

Married in Montana

His Promise
Love's Promise
A Promise of Forever

The Parker Sisters

Thrill of the Chase
The Dating Game
Play Hard to Get
What We Can't Have
Go Your Own Way
A June Wedding

Kate & Walker
One Night
Edge of Night
Last Night

Walk the Right Road Series
The Choice
Lost and Found
Merkaba
Bounty
Blown Away: The Final Chapter

The Saved Series
Saved
Vanished
Captured

Single Titles
He Came Back
Loving Christine

For my German Readers
Die Außenseiter-Reihe
Der Vergessene Junge
Der Gefallene Held

For my French Readers
L'ENFANT OUBLIÉ